THE
DARK KNIGHTS
SUNRISE

The Outcast of the Dark Knight Series

II

YENPRI LAYPIL

Yenpri Laypil

Disclaimer

Outcast of the Dark Knight is a work of fiction. Names, characters, places, and incidents either are the products of the author's imagination or are used fictitiously. Any resemblance to actual persons, living or dead, businesses, companies, events, or locales is entirely coincidental. Opinions and beliefs expressed by the characters do not reflect the author's opinions and beliefs. This book is intended for adults. It contains scenes of graphic violence, creative language and sexual innuendo. It does not contain explicit sexual content.

BOOKS IN THE OUTCAST SERIES

BOOK ORDER IN THE OUTCAST SERIES

CHRONOLOGY: All stories in the Outcast of the Dark Knight series are shown in chronological order as follows:

The Dark Knights Return

The Dark Knights Sunrise

The Dark Knights Ascend

The Dark Knights Inferno

The Dark Knights Awaken

The Dark Knights Hero

BOOKS IN THE OUTCAST BOXSET SERIES

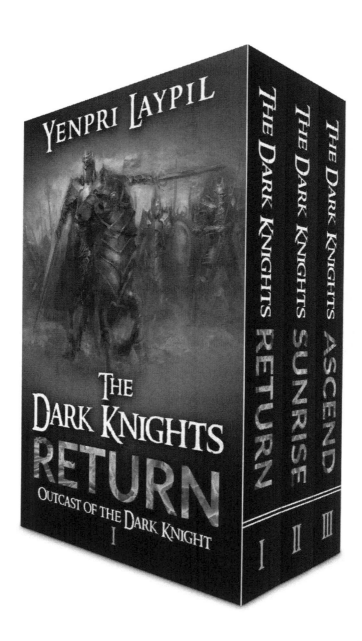

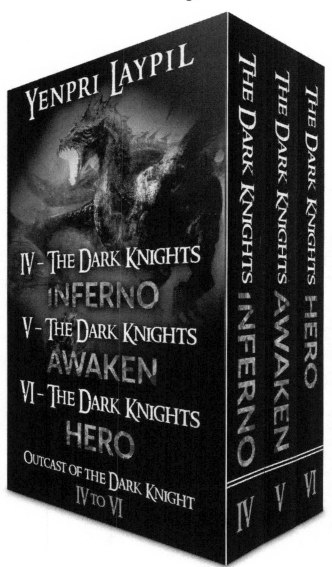

Yenpri Laypil

BOOK ORDER IN THE OUTCAST BOXSET SERIES

CHRONOLOGY: All stories in the Outcast of the Dark Knight series are shown in chronological order as follows:

Boxset 1: Books 1-3

Boxset 2: Books 4-6

ALSO BY SERENITY PETERSON & YENPRI LAYPIL

$\mathcal{A}$cknowledgements

Ah! Hello there, it's great to see you again. Are you ready for more? This is only really the beginning for our warriors. I dedicate this book to you in appreciation of your encouragement for "free-spirited thinking" and a sense of adventure. As the great Geoffrey Chaucer (played by Paul Bettany) remarked in "A Knight's Tale" with my own flavor, "And so without further gilding the lily and with no more ado, I give to you, the seeker of serenity, the protector of Barbarian virginity, the enforcer of our Lord God, the one, the only…

able of Contents

Bellorus's Breakthrough

Where in the world is Valkin at a time like this?

The Fields of Iriseae

When Valkin meets the master

The beach house and the awakening of Valkin Kendor

The Fall of Volcanock

Horses and wolves

Fear of tears

The Master unleashed

The twist in the tale

What's important to you?

The code of battle

The Dark martial arts of life and war

Showdown at Gilipriel

The code of battle is invoked

Rehowlor vs. Valkin

BOOKS IN THE OUTCAST SERIES

BOOK ORDER IN THE OUTCAST SERIES

BOOKS IN THE OUTCAST BOXSET SERIES

BOOK ORDER IN THE OUTCAST BOXSET SERIES

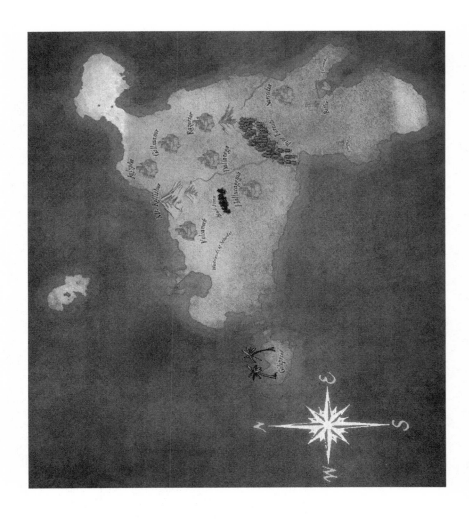

Prologue

Valkin Kendor is beginning to learn who he really is. The farm boy from Tillmandor has grown much since his capture by the King of the Barbarians, Vallentor, now trained in the mysterious arts beyond the realms of magic and science, and not a moment too soon for the war against the kingdom of Sarcodia is looming! King Braithwaite of Sarcodia extends an invite to the infamous gauntlet contest for the prize of a kiss from his beautiful daughter, Princess Melody, and 20,000 Zafrith. The opportunity is too hard to resist for Valkin…

$\mathcal{E}$ngaged & almost ready to play

"Okay gentlemen, so the knight games in Bellor are now over and it's about time we have some real fun watching the poor things risk their lives in the deadly gauntlet. What do you say about that, Prince Michael?" asked King Marcus Braithwaite with a snug smile on his face as he sat on his large central throne with forearms crossed.

Marcus, King Marcus Braithwaite, King of Sarcodia and leader of the Sarcodian people beamed an unnaturally, powerful and deep voice across the great halls of Gillmanor. His cool, confident demeanor blew through his long, twisted hickory brown hair with the wind brought along the surface of the land from the east.

Prince Michael on the other hand was not a king and for bloody good reason. It was a title that he was simply not worthy of. What a wuss! He was like a sausage without the meat in it, just the intestinal lining of an undernourished sheep on its last breath. There was neither substance nor any point to this man, other than the fact that he was the only adopted son to King Gilleus of Gillmanor and heir to the throne. This middle-pathed blond-haired, green-eyed, fair-complexion idiot of a man bore a usual average height of who gives a shit, scrawny built with no effect whatsoever. He was always wearing his fluffy marmalade orange royal robes and was spoilt rotten to his rotten core. He never lifted a sword in

14

his life; in fact, he struggled to lift the breakfast knife to his small, useless mouth. The women of the lands often wondered if he managed to get anything up at all. He couldn't kill a wine goblet fly for the fly was more likely to incapacitate him first by sitting on his head agitating him enough to cause him to hit and knock himself out cold in the process. The women of the lands dreamt of those wonderful and charming princes that they could one day get married to; unfortunately, they would have to dream on if they were considering Prince Michael.

"Well, I say. That's a splendid idea good king! Absolutely splendid! Round up the best knights you have for running the infamous gauntlet. The prize shall naturally be a kiss from Gillmanor's future queen," said Prince Michael in a squeaky tone of voice that made poor Princess Melody Braithwaite cringe in her seat situated next to her father.

She wore a beautiful, silky sapphire blue dress that was pleated with stars that sparkled in the morning sunlight. She sat with her arms folded in disapproval of the terrible predicament she found herself in. She crossed her legs tightly in disgust and stress. However, the rich color of her dress was dulled by her low mood, which weighed her down like a ton of ashblock.[1]

"Awww! Come on Prince Michael, is that all the winner gets?" laughed King Braithwaite cynically as he turned to face his daughter sitting right next to him who smiled a fake smile hiding an uneasy, sickening feeling deep within her. King Braithwaite's voice was deep and strong and his stomach was filled with a dirty beard with wine and breadcrumbs from the sumptuous breakfast they had just indulged in. It was a stark contrast from his "alter-ego", which was a well-muscled, well-oiled frightening figure, one of great strength and power. His daughter was not amused and did not acknowledge her father's insult as she sat motionless and expressionless next to his broad left-hand side.

"I'm afraid so. It's all I can spare for now good King, for I want your daughter all for myself," replied Prince Michael with a sadistic smile on his face rubbing his hands as he looked at King Braithwaite and then at Princess Melody. Melody just kept her gaze forward overlooking the kingdom as the cold, slithery grey wall behind her started to wrap itself

---

[1] Ashblock was a stone found deep in the mountains of Volcanock. It was extremely durable and difficult to penetrate by most.

around her in a vice-grip that did not want to let her go. Suddenly, her petite 5.2 ft frame felt small and insignificant amongst the heavyweights that surrounded her.

"Haha! Don't forget, that she will always be my daughter, young Prince," replied the Sarcodian King with strength in his bone-crushing voice as he scrutinized Prince Michael's diabolical intentions with his cedar-dark brown eyes and tanned eyebrows. King Braithwaite had not shaved for many days now and resembled a man far older than his true age, which intensely intimidated both Prince Michael and his father King Gilleus.

Prince Michael returned a lukewarm smile back at the King of Kings as he retreated back into his smaller fit-for-a-Prince chair knowing full well that the South Eastern kingdom could crush them at any time.

The elegantly crafted table before them was rectangular and covered with a blood wine maroon cloth trimmed with a golden stained edge of royalty. It was excessively filled with exotic meat dishes from far and wide, as well as fruits and desserts and freshly squeezed juices from the ripe nectar produced by the Gillmanorian farms. They were snuggly seated upon the castle's breakfast balcony, which overlooked the entire kingdom of Gillmanor.

Princess Melody was not hungry this morning and understandably so. She was seated next to her future husband who was an imbecile. His presence alone was enough to put her appetite off completely! The thought of spending the rest of her life with a witless, fool was almost unbearable but she held her composure well in front of her future in-laws. She had no other choice but to. She understood her sovereign purpose. She never agreed to it but what could she do, she thought. She was just a puppet that spoke when told to do so and even thought when told to do so. Such was the nature of the women's purpose in such a chauvinistic society where her purpose was tailored to lever peaceful political takeovers as opposed to hostile ones. Princess Melody succumbed to her sad reality.

Her father sat next to her on her right with King Gilleus and his stunning wife Alekto sitting next to him.

King Gilleus, King of Gillmanor was a hazy blue-eyed king with a keen interest in cementing an alliance with his southernmost allies of Sarcodia. His cloud white and aged grey beard was fashioned into the beak of a falcon which curved into his cheek. His wrinkled features showed prowess, age, and cunning wisdom. His thin and athletic frame was full after its indulgence in the delicious morning treats laid out before him by his servants. Gillmanor's royal robe colors were that of a sunset orange encrusted with a red halo stained with blood; and so, King Gilleus's robes honored the traditions of his kingdom and so did his wife, Alekto.

Alekto was one of the most beautiful queens around. Although dwarfed by her husband's 5 ft 9-inch height, she wasn't young but she didn't look old either. She was so ravishingly beautiful, so much so, that King Braithwaite at times, found it very difficult not to stare at certain regions of her voluptuous body. She had a perfect tan and curvy features that fit well with her bright cherry red dress that she donned upon this glorious morning. The only problem for King Braithwaite and the like was that she was a bit of a snob, an attribute sometimes expected with some pompous royalty. Those voluptuous curves of her well-defined body and her equally matched attitude made her a queen to die for. Only Princess Melody could give her a run for her copious amounts of money in terms of shallow beauty. Princess Melody was just as gorgeous with her curly black locks and puffed dimples; although underdeveloped in certain areas she remained an outstanding figure with vast potential for "improvement" in the eyes of the sick-minded.

The Gillmanorian council members were also seated at the table in less glamorous attire and were delighted at the gauntlet idea and immediately set off to prepare for the great event that has hurt and crippled many a man; but for Princess Melody, getting hurt was certainly a small price to pay for an illustrious kiss from her heavenly lips. There was no comparison and no better gift than that!

Poor Melody! She just sat there leaning on her right arm resting her weary head on her lifeless hands staring blankly into the distance whilst all the other royal members talked their pompous heads off. Despite the futility of the situation, she knew for certain that Prince Michael at least would not be kissing her anytime soon and she took comfort in that thought. She would rather kiss an animal for an animal would love her more unconditionally than he would, she thought. She almost vomited her half-eaten breakfast at the thought of kissing the vile creature that Prince Michael was, but the one thing that no one could rob from her was her thoughts and hearing. Through her bondage, she heard ideas and thoughts of how soon the wedding will be. She heard whispers about the impending war against the barbarians of Hallucagenia. Then, she thought about Valkin and how she tried to kill him and as she did, her eyes slowly closed with regret as she sat up straight. She wished she had, for she wondered how different her fate could have been. She wondered for a while and then rested her head on her left arm and opened her eyes again and frowned.

King Braithwaite astutely noticed all of this and shook his head frowning only for a moment and then returned to the mundane conversation with a false smile and sense of security upon his rough face. He talked for a few moments to King Gilleus and then stopped. A silent stroke of fear collided with his consciousness as a look of mild concern overcame his face. With cedar dark brown eyes, he gazed into the distance.

King Gilleus immediately saw this familiar look upon his colleague's face as King Braithwaite turned to face the very front of the Gillmanorian kingdom.

Something or someone was coming...

The rage of Tereartre Levon

"Have you placed the garrison at the Gillmanor Gates, Gilleus?" asked a very mildly concerned King Braithwaite with a deep and strong voice as his colleague started to breathe more heavily.

Queen Alekto was very concerned at how stiff her husband had suddenly become and wondered what was going on as goosebumps started to populate her breasts leaving bumps of rolling outgrowths on her near-perfect skin.

Suddenly, a thunderous clap filled the air with shock and fear! The now terrified royalty quivered in their chairs after the loud sound rang true through the air.

"Father, what was that?" asked an extremely worried Melody with a look of dread upon her pale face.

"That my lovely daughter is the sound of vengeance!" King Braithwaite smiled but remained cool as he looked at his daughter and placed a reassuring palm upon her face. "You should get our future in-laws inside darling. King Gilleus and I will take care of this. Go now!"

King Braithwaite was not perturbed as Melody motioned for Alekto and Prince Michael to follow her inside as another loud crash filled the air with deafening fear.

"His energy levels are so weak I can barely sense him, my Lord. Could it be him after all of that?" asked King Gilleus with a profound and hoarse voice as he faced forward to now what seemed like an explosion of smoke rising from the main gates of Gillmanor's entrance to the kingdom.

King Braithwaite smiled and looked at King Gilleus.

"Come now, Gilleus, don't you recognize your old friends, or has your time basking in royalty dulled your Knightean senses? I suggest you shed your ridiculous robes for something a bit more comfortable. We are going to have a bit of a dangerous and angry encounter very soon."

Smoke rose from the rusty, dusty gates of Gillmanor as two more thunderous clangs rocked the rusty charcoal hinges and weakened locks preventing whatever lay before it from entering. The wooden doors, reinforced with two layers of wood and iron, were locked with a solid piece of oak that could only be lifted with a lever and pulley system. The small garrison placed to defend the door was slowly increasing and more so after the second clang splintered the wooden lock just barely preventing the two gates from flying open now.

King Braithwaite and King Gilleus watched in silence upon the balcony as a third loud crash sounded and was followed by another final crashing sound as if something large had just fallen over after putting up a brave defense.

They looked at each other and smiled as the screams sounded from down below. Birds flew away from the smoke in a flurry of fear and haste.

The wooden lock had splintered and opened with such explosive force that it sent shards of woody daggers toward the garrison stationed at the gates impaling a few Gillmanorian warriors donned with orange and red elite armor. As the others helplessly watched their comrades fall lifelessly to the ground next to them, the lucky ones who survived wondered, if they too would survive whatever was going to walk through that gate. They stood firm nonetheless. Then, the largest Werethallic wolf that the younger warriors had ever seen, pounced in front of them catching them by surprise. It grabbed two men in its snout crushing them instantly allowing their lifeless bodies to roll out from its salivating mouth. Two tons of brown tufts of grey and white with patches of faint black strands of fur here and there sauntered into the Gillmanorian kingdom bearing a green-cloaked rider with an insignia from the forbidden Pine forests. The somber rider held the brown leather reins of his menacing wolven companion and looked around striking fear into the very hearts of the king's guard. They tried to resist.

"ARCHERS, AIM!" shouted one of the commanders.

The mysterious warrior knew exactly what was going to happen as the archers stationed upon the gate watchtowers were about to let loose a shower of arrows upon him.

The rider calmly jumped off from his wolf and then walked towards the warriors before him protected only by an olive green breastplate and silver gauntlets. The warrior then banged his head with a closed fist releasing a thunderous clap in the process that reverberated through the very core of the warriors causing them to stagger back a bit.

The elite warriors charged with guarding the gate took a reluctant step back as the strange warrior proceeded to withdraw a fiery sword from his forehead concealed by his green cloak. His cloak eventually could not withstand the searing heat of the sword and eventually caught alight and burned away quite quickly.

The Gillmanorian general shouted, "FIRE!" The warriors atop the watchtower let loose the first wave of arrows upon the strange fiery warrior whose face was now completely revealed. It was the Werethallic King of the Pine forests in the South himself, Tereartre Levon. Tears stained his dirty, bloodied face as he stood there silently waiting for the arrows to strike his body. His neon green eyes were closed as he paused and then decided to open them allowing the fire of the Dark Knight within him to ooze and float just above his head.

Intense horror flooded through every warrior being who gazed upon him. Some have heard the stories of the king of the forest. They believed that he was a peaceful man who did not seek war and therefore no one had anticipated finally meeting him in this manifestation.

Many arrows struck Tereartre Levon but he was undisturbed and unperturbed. He just continued his blank, fiery gaze at the warriors. Suddenly, without warning the arrows caught alight and burned away to the wind. The gaping wounds within Tereartre's body soon sealed completely to the amazement of the warriors. Tereartre Levon then lifted his sword and asked, "Where is Braithwaite?" in the lowest, most unlike tone of voice that he could muster.

No one uttered a word.

Tereartre was growing very impatient now. "TELL ME!" he then shouted startling the warriors before him.

"STAND FIRM MEN!" commanded their General as he stepped forward to meet Tereartre Levon head-on. "I am General Whitaker of the king's guard. I will answer your questions." General Whitaker was a seasoned veteran within the king's guard, a man who fought and survived the great barbarian war and who defected from the Sarcodian army to join Gillmanor. He was considered a war hero in Gillmanorian history. He walked right up to Tereartre Levon.

"Now, wha...!" General Whitaker did not complete his question to Tereartre finding Tereartre's sword lodged right through his torso. Tereartre withdrew his fiery sword from General Whitaker allowing the good General to fall lifelessly to his knees and then forward, face first into the ground to the shock and horror of his speechless men. Tereartre then roared with anger.

The garrison was now also filled with anger and they were all fired up after witnessing their general's death that they decided with the fall of their hero, they would avenge his death, but little did they know who it was they were about to face.

"COME!" smiled Tereartre wearing earthly brown leather pants as he surged forward cleaving through the hordes of elite soldiers that tried to kill him. As he fought them, pieces of fiery armor singed with dark coals flew in from nowhere stunning the Gillmanorian soldiers and sometimes knocking them out cold. The pieces proceeded to fuse to Tereartre's weary and tired body. He roared and screamed with pain as the armor painfully burned him as it fused to his body. He became stronger and stronger with each armor piece that flew in. He was transforming into a Dark Knight! His body temperature was rapidly increasing emitting a searing pulse of heat preventing any warrior from now getting into the kill zone.

Rufor Rafelieus, the Werethallic king wolf circled Tereartre making sure no warrior decided to do anything stupid and attack him from behind.

Tereartre now stood with eyes peering into the sea of bodies that lay before him. His Dark Knight Helmet did not yet fly in. A foolish young warrior decided enough was enough and he was going to attack

Tereartre, but to his surprise, Tereartre's Dark Knight Helmet flew in knocking the man behind his head cracking his skull killing him instantly and fusing with Tereartre's head. The helmet was first cold and sedentary and then suddenly, it became fiery red-hot emitting a flamethrower of fire from the eye slits that peered into the lonely sky.

Rufor smiled as he knew his master has just unleashed his truest form on the Gillmanorians.

Kings Braithwaite and Gilleus did not like what they felt and collectively took off their robes and jumped off the twenty-foot-tall balcony.

Tereartre stabbed the ground with his black fire sword and goaded the warriors to come at him, which they very reluctantly did. The first one tried to swing his sword but Tereartre punched him so hard, that his fist went right through the man leaving a gaping hole right through him. Tereartre was in a killing frenzy trance-like state. Every warrior that came at him ended up dead or incapacitated. Tereartre did not grace their deaths with the use of his sword. Perhaps, he did not deem them worthy enough to die by it. He was so angry that his attributes of respect and honor were completely clouded by an inner storm that refused to subside.

Suddenly, two warriors appeared before him to the relief of the king's guard. Tereartre's hand was stuck right through a man's body but once these two warriors appeared, his attention was captured by their presence and he flung the body of the lifeless man away to focus solely on them.

"King Braithwaite, and his puppet Gilleus!" remarked Tereartre in a low sadistic voice. "YOU FOOLS! You have no idea what you are doing. You are tearing these lands apart with this feud. YOU HAVE PUSHED ME TOO FAR! YOU MADE ME KILL A FRIEND! A FRIEND, Raaarrrrrr!" exclaimed Tereartre with anger and rage as he picked up his fiery sword from the ground with great speed and rushed towards King Braithwaite in a flurry of olive green singed armor.

King Braithwaite saw him coming but just stood still. He was unphased by his advance and closed his eyes allowing Tereartre to advance towards him with an overcut intending to slice King Braithwaite in two. Clang! A shiny silver sword glinting in the noon sunlight prevented Tereartre's fiery blade from cutting King Braithwaite into two halves. To Tereartre's surprise, he found King Gilleus's blade blocking his own from reaching its intended target, that of King Braithwaite. King Braithwaite smiled as Tereartre and Gilleus were caught in a bind, which lasted a few seconds with Tereartre withdrawing first and retreating backward. King Gilleus held his ground with a defensive front guard.

Tereartre was not amused.

Elsewhere, a smoke-grey-eyed warrior opened his eyes with worry and concern from an afternoon's deep contemplation. He stood up with horror from his royal throne in a royal hut and stormed through the great doors towards the kingdom's farms. He was running fast enough so that his barbarian comrades could see him coming and they respectfully stepped out of the way to allow him to pass. As he was running, he shed his golden royal robe and retained only his brown cloak underneath. Ominous eyes followed his movements after a non-verbal exchange between each other. The inner barracks gates clanged open as the king of Hallucagenia ran through marking a trail of disturbed dust. The barbarians stepped aside as he made his pathway. He then leaped above the outer barracks gates before they could creak open in haste. Two brothers who patrolled the forest line saw the king and quietly slipped away into the Pine forests with detection.

"Why do you shield such a corrupt man, Gilleus?" asked Tereartre with a disappointed tone in his crackling and unsure voice.

"I'm not protecting him; I'm protecting my Kingdom and my people. You come here uninvited! You callously kill my men! What treatment did you expect Tereartre for your uncharacteristic behavior? I am shocked and disappointed!" King Gilleus aired his feelings expressing his disapproval of the situation.

Tereartre roared and advanced once again toward King Gilleus who shook his head in disappointment. Tereartre attacked Gilleus with a barrage of over and undercuts, which the Gillmanorian king easily deflected away with one hand. Tereartre's burning eyes and black sword were slowly becoming weary and misdirected. He was losing energy fast and Rufor barked at him from behind in a vain effort to spur him on. The warrior spirit within Tereartre then decided to eke out one last desperate assault.

However, when Tereartre attacked, he found himself exposed and King Gilleus exploited that opening neutralizing his offense.

Tereartre eked out a final thrust to King Gilleus's torso which King Gilleus dodged by simply stepping aside allowing the fiery blade to only just pass his torso and out of harm's way. King Gilleus then caught Tereartre's gauntlet and squeezed it firmly crushing it slightly.

Tereartre roared in pain as he felt the armor pierce into his flesh releasing a flood of blood that soiled his Dark Knight armor. He felt the strength from his body slowly and painfully slip away and he could no longer maintain his grip on his sword. He let go! It fell slowly in defeat to the ground and as it hit the earth, its once bright flame soon extinguished itself returning to its usual calmer silver sheen.

A sparkling tear fell from Rufor's eye bearing the reflection of King Gilleus's right hand slapping Tereartre's helmet clean off from his head revealing his former bloodied and tired face to all.

Tereartre's eyes were still on fire as he breathed heavily. Tereartre couldn't fight back. King Gilleus's sword was lodged right through his left hand as well. Blood began to drip from Tereartre's arm, as did the tears from Rufor's defeated eyes.

Gillmanorian men started to enclose the wolven leader in an enveloping circle but Rufor did not flinch a muscle in response to his impending capture.

King Gilleus removed his sword from Tereartre's arm as Tereartre gasped in pain looking up at him with defeat.

King Braithwaite stood still and then folded his arms lifting his head with pride and with a smug smirk upon his face at the ease with which his colleague had dispatched the minor threat of Tereartre Levon.

"Finish him off, Gilleus. He longer wishes to join us in our realization," commanded the beaming voice of King Braithwaite.

King Gilleus turned around to shortly face him and took a deep breath and then sighed in disappointment as he fixed his gaze upon the bloody and beaten Tereartre who was staring an empty and defeated stare of despair and depression.

He didn't even see King Gilleus start to walk toward him to finish him off.

Suddenly, the illuminating figure of Vallentor appeared in front of the defeated frame of Tereartre along with Marve and Raven Ominous, the Death brothers flanking the barbarian king.

"MARVE!" shouted Vallentor. "WATCH IT!"

King Braithwaite traversed a hundred-foot distance between himself and his enemies with his long sword drawn and ready to kill. He threw a deadly flat snap against Marve intending to take his head clean off along with Tereartre's and Vallentor's heads. The opportunity was too enticing for King Braithwaite to miss.

Marve instinctively had his sword drawn and held it tightly with his two hands bracing himself for impact but Marve knew he was no match for the mighty King of Sarcodia. With balls of sweat streaming down his tanned dark face, he knew that King Braithwaite's immense power was going to overcome him with one strike. Marve held his sword as tightly and as strongly as he possibly could. Impact! Shockwaves of the devastating blow sent the Gillamanorian elites backward covering their faces and preventing the sand particulates from clouding their already blurred vision of this epic fight as King Braithwaite's sword struck Marve's short black assassin sword.

King Braithwaite's sword was a broad cold steel grey sword, specially constructed for King Braithwaite to maximize the deadly force he puts behind his blows. Weighing in at nearly 260 lb, the sword was nearly as heavy as its master. King Braithwaite liked to inflict slower more devastating blows to his foes. He enjoyed it more!

The Sarcodian King's power was just too much for Marve to contain causing Marve's minuscule double-edged sword to screech and falter backward towards his head starting to lightly cut into his forehead.

Vallentor saw this ruthless attack unfolding and intervened with a defensive deflection using his shimmering silver-edged sword driving hard upon King Braithwaite's attack widening the shockwaves of energy being emitting from the deadly flat-snap by the Sarcodian King. However, it still was not enough to neutralize the attack of the huge frame of the mighty King Braithwaite. The looks upon Vallentor and Marves' faces changed from determination to stressful intensity realizing that their combined power was not enough. They try and hold on for a little longer but were desperately running out of energy.

King Braithwaite bore a vengeful look that began to change into one of sheer cruelty as he gritted a sadistic smile upon his face knowing he had the upper hand.

Sweat and pain began to flow through the weary bodies of Vallentor and Marve as a look of horror overcame Raven's face. He knew his comrades were in big trouble and decided to step in. Tiptoeing towards the heart of the defense, he withdrew his pitch-black assassin sword and readied himself. He caught King Braithwaite unaware launching a driving uppercut attempting to deflect King Braithwaite's strike.

A third shockwave blasted through the air sending more dust and unsettling winds toward the shaken Gillmanorian elites who now had to fully cover their eyes. The sounds of three screeching swords fighting against a lone broadsword reverberated in the very core of their frightened souls as they stood contemplating the immense power of the individuals battling before them.

King Braithwaite did not expect the surprise deflection from Raven and could feel his sword being slowly driven upwards and out of harm's way.

Furry hair began to grow out from Raven's arms as he drove his sword upwards with a flicker of widening yellow light in his determined orange eyes gritting his teeth and clenching his midnight assassin attire.

King Braithwaite's sword was finally deflected, as he succumbed to the indignation of the fight, above the heads of the three warriors. He was then momentarily blinded by his hand covering his angry vision.

This opening was cleverly exploited by the warriors who jumped backward to prevent King Braithwaite's follow-up attack which was a crosscut across the torso. King Braithwaite missed to his surprise.

"RUFOR, TEREARTRE, JUMP, JUMP, JUMP!!!" shouted Vallentor to a wary Rufor who sprung into action grabbing Tereartre by the scruff of his neck and jumping over the gates of Gillmanor in a single leap. The three warriors stood with front guards facing King Braithwaite's gritted teeth of frustration. Raven and Marve backflipped towards the gate and jumped over it whilst Vallentor and King Braithwaite stood staring at each other contemplating their next meeting.

King Braithwaite's stern and focused face overruled Vallentor's dispensation of madness. As Vallentor backtracked, King Braithwaite threw his sword into the air and allowed it to fuse with his back sheath signifying his recognition of Vallentor's retreat. King Braithwaite then lifted his hand showing Vallentor the way out, pointing towards the gate, which Vallentor gladly ascended with a single leap.

Marve, Raven, and Rufor along with the broken and battered body of Tereartre were already well on the way to Hallucagenia.

Vallentor joined them and as he looked back at the Kingdom of Gillamanor. Concern and worry overcame his rough face as he refocused his attention on his battered comrade.

*W*hat happened atop Mt. Killithur?

"WHY?" shouted Vallentors as he tightly grabbed onto Tereartre's emerald green tunic lifting him completely off the ground with one hand against the wall gritting his teeth with anger and frustration. "YOU RISKED YOUR OWN BLOODY LIFE, THE LIVES OF YOUR COMRADES TO GO AFTER BRAITHWAITE ALONE! FOR REVENGE! ARE YOU CRAZY?" shouted Vallentor with an angry tone of voice that echoed throughout the royal hallways of Hallucagenia.

Raven and Marve stood in solemn silence with low bowed heads as their comrade accepted the shouts and barrage of lethal questions that pierced his heart and mind.

Rufor's head was bowed low as he too was implicated in violating Vallentor's direct orders and awaited his turn next.

Tereartre's head took the punishment with anguish and defeat knowing that he had made a grave mistake. His brown leather pants were stained with blood and so was his heavy heart.

Vallentor did not afford him the luxury of a fresh change of clothes for he felt he didn't deserve it after his vengeful antics earlier on today. "AND YOU!" turned Vallentor to face the defeated frame of Rufor Rafelieus who slunk down to all fours and buried his head within his huge pearl white paws.

Vallentor wagged his hand. He transformed from a doting big brother into a caring father speaking to his naughty son who just did something terribly wrong.

Rufor further slunk into his paws in fear.

"I CAN'T BELIEVE YOU ALLOWED THIS TO HAPPEN AFTER ALL OF THAT BLOODSHED! I MEAN, WHAT WERE YOU TWO THINKING? LET'S JUST WALTZ INTO GILLMANOR AND TAKE ON GILLEUS, GILLEUS, AND HOPE TO SURVIVE THAT, AND THEN TAKE ON BRAITHWAITE. I MEAN COME ON!"

Rufor shed a light blue tear that trickled down his furry face expressing his inner sadness and pain. His fire-orange eyes peered away from his "father" as he scolded him further.

"REVENGE WILL NOT HEAL YOUR WOUNDS. IT WILL ONLY GET YOU KILLED SOONER!" Vallentor's cynicism intertwined with his frustration and anger as he shook his head in disappointment. He released his grip upon Tereartre who fell back down to earth and started to walk towards the royal meeting room leaving them behind to catch up.

The four warriors follow his hurried footsteps with heads bowed low and stressed intensity upon their faces. No words were exchanged between them.

Vallentor blasted through the meeting room doors and immediately slunk himself into his royal chair at the head of the triangle resting one of his tired legs on the dark oak armrests.

The royal meeting room was unusually dark today with only the simmering charcoal yellow light of the torches and fireplace bringing illumination into the room. The dark maroon curtains juxtaposed with the volcanock dune colored walls were rarely drawn in the meeting room, which was an old barbarian custom to maintain the secrecy of the discussions held within. Old relics were placed upon the mantelpiece above the raging fire below as crossed swords mounted upon the brilliant yellow wall stood firm in the silence of the room. The scent of smoke filled the air with a thick and heavy ambiance making it difficult to breathe at times.

"SIT DOWN AND START TALKING!" demanded King Vallentor with authority and no-nonsense in his voice.

Tereartre slowly walked to his chair and tentatively sat down upon it, peering into the reflection of the torches upon the glass top of the elegant mahogany triangular table.

Behind Tereartre stood a wall-mounted barbarian axe and shield as tributes to former barbarian kings slain in battle.

Raven and Marve also sat down. Raven sat on Vallentor's right and Marve to his left whilst Rufor nestled himself by the cozy comforting fire still sweating from the midday's bloody affairs.

Tereartre then lifted his head to face Vallentor and started to relate his story.

Vallentor and the others listen intently as Tereartre related every sordid detail, in a soft and sad voice, of what he believed to have happened. The warriors' heads turned at times and bowed low with great sadness as they heard his words fall upon their heavily loaded hearts. Tereartre finished his side of the story leaving the room with more silence and coldness than what it originally had.

Vallentor was the first to break the icy silence with an avalanche. "I cannot believe this!" he exclaimed. Vallentor, whose fiery dispensation seems to have simmered into one of more reason, got up from his chair at the point of the triangular table and walked towards the roaring fire beside him with his cream robes and golden brown embroidery holding his chin in deep thought as he leaned upon the finely crafted mantelpiece. Rufor put his head down in sadness as Vallentor stood towering above what normally was the huge frame of a wolf on any other day but today the imposing figure of Rufor was reduced to a small insignificant hound.

Raven and Marve clenched their fists and gnawed away at the inner acorns of their mouths.

Tereartre had a look of stone upon his tired face as he wiped off the mixture of sweat and blood that was now dripping down the side of his exhausted visage. He didn't bother to clean himself since the war of the woods. The green stubble upon his chin and cheeks was evident of a man who just didn't care anymore. Only out of necessity, he understood that he had to report back to Vallentor as soon as possible and so he made for the kingdom of Hallucagenia with haste but something snapped within him. Rufor could do nothing to either ameliorate the situation or dissuade Tereartre from his course of action.

"It is true, Vallentor. Many friends were killed on that terrible night by my own hands. I was only giving in to my true feelings of anger and revenge for which I profusely apologize to you and the council," remarked Tereartre as he stood up and bowed low with his trembling left hand across his chest in a gesture of forgiveness.

Vallentor immediately acknowledged this and traversed the great distance between himself and Tereartre to hold his shoulders reassuringly.

"Your apology is accepted, my good friend." Vallentor smiled at Tereartre who also smiled in recognition.

Rufor popped up his head and also smiled feeling that the worst was over between friends but slowly rested his head down knowing that the worst was yet to come between enemies.

Vallentor went back to the mantelpiece and contemplated Tereartre's actions further with an air of curiosity, which Tereartre saw fit to answer.

"Vallentor, the serpent's leer has been employed and that can only mean one thing!"

Goosebumps of fear ran through Raven and Marve's consciousness, whilst the possibility still registered in the mind of Vallentor as he peered into the simmering fire. He then turned around to face Tereartre with sadness and devastation clenching his fists in a fit of empathetic anger and rage.

"ARGGH! He's gotten to them. The bastard's got to them." Vallentor's anger was apparent as he continued his stare into the fire.

"Poor Magnus, for all these years, he honored that treaty, and for what! We just can't get a break, can we? With every bloody moment that passes, he gets another fucking alliance and we draw closer to defeat," said Marve clenching his fists. The tall 6.5 ft man masked his height as he sat still trying to contain his seething anger.

"Calm down, Marve. Getting angry won't do us any good," cautioned Raven as he shifted his gaze toward Vallentor. "What do you make of it, king?" asked Raven.

Vallentor turned around to face Raven and the others.

"Well, the Serpentines have clearly made their choice and the forest gorillas have paid dearly for it. It was a smart plan to enslave them with the serpent's leer and let them lose in our territory. In a way, this attack has revealed a part of Braithwaite's plan. He's clearing out the forests to

32

make way for his grand march into the kingdom. Setting the gorillas loose upon the Werethall was a brilliant plan. Tererartre's man and wolf numbers were severely depleted in the attack. Simple and smart, just like Braithwaite! I hope whoever is left has escaped the leer and fled from the forests to the quieter northern or southern parts for now. Our eastern shields are on the very brink of failure."

Tereartre bowed his head low in disappointment as Vallentor laid out the bare facts to the council and feelings of regret filled his soul knowing that he could have done more to assist.

"But it's not the Serpentines, nor the gorillas, nor even Rehowlor that's bothering me." Vallentor leaned on the table and looked at his commanders who were confused now. They all looked at each other wondering what Vallentor was talking about. What could possibly be more of a concern than these issues at hand they wondered? He then laughed loudly and replied, "I'm worried about who's going to win the gauntlet contest and get to kiss our beloved Princess Melody tomorrow. That's what I'm worried about."

Raven covered his face of former horror with shame, as he believed that there was something very important that Vallentor was going to say.

Marve, on the other hand, was in stitches rolling upon the floor with laughter next to Rufor who was also laughing and barking loudly.

The entire mood of the conversation changed and altered its course towards a lighter, less beaten road.

Everyone was laughing. Even Tereartre had a small smile on his face. He welcomed and appreciated the change in the subject that effectively took the tension out of the situation.

Vallentor knew exactly what he was doing. "Right, Raven, Marve, I believe our young man is ready and has an inkling as to what is about to happen to him."

"Well, we did mention a contest, an engagement, and an unveiling but that's all we told him," replied the Ominous brothers collectively with great big smiles on their faces.

"Great stuff brothers! That's perfect! Now Rufor, you're going to go to the magister temple," smiled Vallentor.

Rufor got up from the fire where he was comfortably sitting and started to shake his furry head in disagreement already.

"ARGH! Come on good king! I hate it when you send me there. I know what's going to happen. I simply must protest! Why don't you send Marve instead this time?" pleaded Rufor.

"HEY! That's not funny," objected Marve who was on his feet now in protestation.

"Now, now Rufor, I know you don't like them and what they do but they need a full creature kind and Marve falls just short in that department or does he? No offense Marve," replied Vallentor as he petted Rufor's head.

"None was taken, my Lord," bowed Marve with a chuckle upon his face as Rufor rolled his eyes in frustration.

"It's just easier to perform the procedure on you as time is running out fast and you are the strongest wolf I know. I'm sorry brother! It's crunch time!" Vallentor rubbed Rufor's head a little more to soften the blow.

Rufor reluctantly nodded in agreement.

"Good! I'm glad we're in agreement. Tereartre…" Tereartre stood firm and awaited his orders. He seemed to have suddenly recovered after Vallentor's change in subject. It seemed to have done him some good. "…what do you know of the sandstone portal?" At the remark of that question, the entire mood in the room changed once again. Everyone froze completely. Only Tereartre focused his thoughts and memories with closed eyes, which he opened only after a few seconds of silent contemplation. He took a deep breath and then exhaled opening his neon green eyes to reply.

"We know it as the Starsand Gates but it is more widely known as the Sandstone Portal. The last time those gates were opened was about twenty-five years ago when we were sent there. I do not know of any other occurrence happening from then until now."

The Death brothers were shocked and stunned momentarily at the fact that Tereartre had some involvement with the sandstone portal.

Raven couldn't help but cut in the conversation, "…You mean to say that you survived everything in there and still stand here today, Tereartre? That is truly an incredible feat! I salute you, sir." Raven bowed to Tereartre with his left hand across his chest in a gesture of respect and admiration.

"I thank you, Raven. It is an interesting place! You should think about going to train there some time," replied Tereartre with a stone look of sincerity face.

"Unbelievable!" exclaimed Raven as Marve admired Tereartre with a new-found look of fear mixed with wonder, awe, and deep respect for the Forest King. The brothers never knew that side of Tereartre's history up until now.

Tereartre smiled as Raven continued his talk of the sandstone portal.

"They say that only the most skilled warriors can survive the challenges in the forbidden lands beyond the gates. The stories that I have heard about that place are unbelievably scary. The intensity of those lands is unparalleled. I too would like to test my strength there someday." Raven seemed determined that one day, he too would travel to the sandstone portal.

"I was very fortunate. I had reached a very high level at the time as a Dark Knight and I had the formidable company of Helleus Kendor to undertake the journey with me. I have to say that if it were not for him, I wouldn't be here to tell you the story."

"What was it like Tereartre?" asked Raven with keen interest. Vallentor didn't mind the curiosity. It was a valuable learning lesson for the Death brothers and the afternoon was still young.

"I can't describe it. It's something that you'll have to experience for yourself to understand it."

Raven and Marve collectively stood up from their chairs and bowed in honor and appreciation of Tereartre's accomplishment.

Tereartre also bowed in appreciation and turned to Vallentor who stood in front of him.

Vallentor then held his shoulder. "My friend, my brother, I'm going to take a chance, perhaps the biggest chance of my life and I need your honest opinion on it. I need everyone's opinion on it." Vallentor paused awkwardly before continuing. "I would like to send Valkin through the sandstone portal." Vallentor then returned his gaze to the mantelpiece allowing everyone to digest his outrageous suggestion. Everyone indeed was taken aback by this preposterous suggestion, especially Tereartre.

Even Rufor who was comfortably sitting on his rug had a look of uneasiness on his face.

Marve was the first to object, "Vallentor, I thought we were killing him enough here. If you put him in there, you'll definitely seal his fate. I didn't have to go there to tell you that. The stories are enough. It's too damn risky for the boy. He wouldn't last ten seconds in there. I wouldn't last ten seconds in there."

Raven and Tereartre were in deep thought and didn't say much until Tereartre shared his thoughts.

"I too share the concerns of Marve here. Valkin is much too young to face the full wrath and magnitude of the forbidden lands beyond the portal. I don't want to sully your plan with my view of realism but at his current level, he'll never make it," said Tereartre plainly and bluntly. Tereartre then turned to face Vallentor. "By sending him in there, his fate will indeed be sealed and he will not return. He's not a warrior yet. The forbidden lands are no place for the weak. It is not a place for mere magicians and normal warriors of the world. The dynasty spares no one, no one! If in a moment your concentration lapses, they will kill you! If you so much as breathe out of sync with the pulse of the portal, it will kill you," said Tereartre with a bleak stare of horror upon his face.

"I fully understand that Tereartre, that is why I'm not sending him in there alone," replied Vallentor to a very concerned Tereartre. "You read my mind, Tereartre Levon. And what's up, Tereartre, you don't like magicians?" asked Vallentor who tried to change the subject. Tereartre looked straight at him and smiled and played along with the change.

"It's not that I don't like them. I just remember clearly what happened to them in the great barbarian war that we fought in." Vallentor was curious and wanted to know more about the war he had never fought in.

"Enlighten me. What actually happened Tereartre?"

"I recall it clearly. It was towards the end of the battle and they were about to cast a revive spell to revive their dead, that is the allied forces of the post-Killithur era. There were about fifty of them. Twenty-five of them were casting the revive spell and the other twenty-five were casting shield spells for themselves and on whatever was left of their infantry and horsemen. The revive spell took effect after about ten seconds so as we killed, ten seconds later, the very same men we slayed behind us were being put back together and revived. As you can imagine, it was the most annoying thing for us to entertain."

Raven and Marve shook their heads in agreement.

"Usually, most armies heavily fortify the Magicians and the great barbarian war was no exception. It was a sea of ranked men protecting one of their most important assets, their Magicians with spears and arrows. It was quite a spectacle to see the circle of men surrounding these "precious" few. Anyway, Helleus and I spotted a weakness on their left flank and we exploited it. We must have cleaved through at least ten thousand men until we reached the bastards. Poor chaps! They looked like a bunch of dead chickens cornered in a chicken run. We pierced through their pathetic magical shields and launched our attack. I think Helleus must have killed about thirty of them by himself, brutally! The last twenty put up a good fight. They tried everything! Every last spell in their bloody magic books but nothing worked. We just stood there and looked at them as they huddled together. They then proceeded to summon every creature they could think of. We systematically killed each one with ease. They then tried a desperation attack, which involved internally exploding themselves in order to kill anything within a ten-mile radius. We thought that was very selfish of them to do, so Helleus and I unleashed the fury of our Hidamen Dark Knight power. The heat incinerated them instantly. Their ashes were blown away with the wind as we chanted our death prayer in respect to them and to those we slayed and were going to slay out of respect. We were soldiers! We had our duty to carry out and we did it well. Please don't misunderstand me. I may hate magicians but I respect the dead and that will never change."

Vallentor shook his head biting his lip as Tereartre concluded.

"I digressed. As I said before, if you send him there, his fate will be sealed. You should send someone capable of protecting him at all times. In fact, I volunteer to go along with him."

Vallentor acknowledged Tereartre's suggestion and turned to face the others.

"Alright gentlemen, Tereartre seems keen to go, but the decision must be unanimous for it to be accepted. Marve?"

Marve looked up at Vallentor and rolled his lips inwards smiling an uneasy smile to his king.

"Well, if Tereartre & Raven are okay with this then I'm okay with it." Marve chuckled as he passed the buck to Raven.

Vallentor smiled and looked at Raven.

"Well, how about it, Raven?" Raven gave out a huge sigh and then lifted his head and smiled. However, Raven had something to say first.

"My suggestion is that we first travel northwest and sail to the Islands near Galapalaus after the completion of the gauntlet games. And finally, may I be considered to accompany Valkin on his journey to and through the sandstone portal."

Tereartre looked at Raven's sudden suggestions with surprise and wondered momentarily before nodding in acknowledgment.

Vallentor also nodded in approval turning to Tereartre.

"Firstly, thank you gentlemen for your willingness to go on this journey with Valkin. Tereartre, I appreciate you wanting to go with Valkin but war is on our doorstep. As much as I would like you to go, I need the Forest King and the Werethallic Force here and now to be our last line of defense against the impending doom that approaches."

"As you wish good king," bowed Tereartre in approval lifting his head with a slight uneasiness in his weakened demeanor.

Vallentor turned to address Raven.

"I like the idea, Raven. I feel I know where you're going with this and it sounds like a good idea to me. How long has it been by the way?" asked Vallentor.

Raven thought for a moment about how long it's been since he last went home.

"Almost twenty-five years now," replied a nostalgic Raven as Marve nodded in agreement going back in time.

"That's a long time. Do you think you'll be able to train him there? There's a lot of memories left in that place?" asked Vallentor with keen interest and genuine concern.

"It will stand us and Valkin in good stead when we eventually enter the sandstone portal. Also, there is arguably no better teacher than the Master himself," answered Raven.

"Ok. I've made my decision. Raven will be the one to accompany Valkin through the sandstone portal. Rufor, what are your thoughts?"

Rufor looked into the fire and then back at Vallentor as Raven slowly digested what Vallentor had just said to him.

"If this is your choice, good king, then the Werethallic WolfKing will stand by your decision."

Vallentor held his chin and looked at Raven signaling to him that the time for contemplation was over and it was now time to decide.

"Raven, how about it? Would you like to be the one?"

Raven took a deep breath raising his right eyebrow creasing the small scar on his left cheek as he did. He then peered across to Vallentor with a gradual smile appearing on his face and then walked up to Vallentor and bowed in acceptance.

"It would be an honor, sir." Raven turned around and silently said "Yes!" to himself.

Marve chuckled at his elder brother.

"Ok great! Everyone, please get to work immediately. I will follow shortly."

All the warriors were about to leave the dark meeting room into the light. Tereartre was the last to leave when Vallentor suddenly called out to him.

"Tereartre, just a moment please."

Tereartre turned around with his blood-stained face and sat down next to Vallentor. The faint tufts of his brilliant green hair were barely visible in the dim light of the room as his head was filled with the filth and blood of the previous day.

Vallentor interlocked his fingers and bowed his head in deep sadness.

The heavy dark brown door closed behind them with a loud thud of finality.

Tereartre gritted his teeth. He hadn't shaved for days. His face was rough with blood-stained stubble that made him look far older than his true age.

"Okay, I know you've got something on your mind, Tereartre. I need to know what it is?" asked Vallentor in a low and ominously, serious voice.

Tereartre looked up at him with a blank look as Vallentor continued. "Look, I know we don't see eye to eye all the time but I genuinely care and I want to know what happened up there." Vallentor seemed genuinely sincere in his request.

Tereartre though, found it strange that Vallentor, a man he hardly knew, actually cared about him. His neon green eyes flinched slightly and then he decided to give Vallentor his opinion.

"I keep thinking about the serpent's leer. It could only have been employed by Arnaiboa, the Serpentine King. I'm not sure how much you know about him, Vallentor?" asked Tereartre with a grave look on his face.

"Not much, stories. I never met the man. They never ventured down towards us in Sarcodia in my time. I do know he was one of the kings that waged war against the Hallucens along with the allied forces."

"That's right. He was also the one who nearly won it for the Allied forces with that attack. Our men switched sides and started attacking us instead, because of the serpent's leer. Trust me when I say this, it's the scariest thing to see your men turn around and start marching the other way towards you. Warriors you laughed with and sparred with just the other day suddenly turned around and tried to kill you. It's a deadly ability, I must say. The attack only works on the weak-minded though. The weak-minded are easy to manipulate and control you see."

That got Vallentor thinking about things.

"Hang on, Tereartre, Magnus was no weak-minded individual. He was thick-headed, yes, but he was strong, very strong," replied a perplexed Vallentor.

"True, but even the strongest can fall. That's why they got him first and then went after the others." Vallentor was confused.

"What do mean, Tereartre?"

"I mean, Arnaiboa himself probably captured him somehow. I suspect that they were aided by King Braithwaithe's son and exposed Magnus to the leer for several days in order to overthrow his mind. After conquering him, the rest would be very simple. I'm sure you've already realized something else as well?" Vallentor shook his head in agreement.

"So they have cleared the forests! Am I right Tereartre?" asked Vallentor to make sure.

"Dead right! The only existing force that patrols and protects the Pine Forests is now my Werethallic Wolf Force. King Braithwaite is preparing to crush us completely and so far, everything is going according to his plan. While he feasts in Gillmanor securing more allies for his rotten cause, we sleep in fear of the day they march into Hallucagenia and take over." Tereartre stood up abruptly and walked towards the door. Vallentor was still seated at the table deep in thought about what Tereartre just said.

Tereartre opened the door and was about to leave the room when Vallentor asked him one final question before he left.

"Why does King Braithwaite want to destroy Hallucagenia so badly Tereartre?" asked Vallentor.

Tereartre stopped in his gait and sighed heavily closing his eyes and looking back at King Vallentor.

"Helleus Kendor killed King Braithwaite's younger brother, Eric." Vallentor immediately stood up with a shock that sent chills down his spine. Tereartre remained silent as he gritted his teeth taking in a deep breath knowing exactly what King Braithwaith was after. Then, it hit Vallentor and he looked at Tereartre also taking a deep breath as Tereartre walked on leaving the door half open.

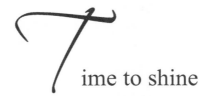

*T*ime to shine

"WHAAAT! No way! That bitch tried to kill me remember! She's pretty, I'll give her that but she's not worth kissing. Besides, she's not my type, it could never work out." Valkin shook his hands in disagreement.

He was wearing his black assassin outfit given to him by his teachers and mentors, Raven and Marve. The subject of their discussions made Valkin particularly uncomfortable even more uncomfortable than he already was feeling. The heat of the day did not help ease the itching feeling that started to crack open his skin. Valkin was sweating even more in the black heat-absorbing outfit with the pressure he was being put under by the Death brothers with all their probing questions.

"Yes Valkin, that's what you'll say now, but just wait until you see her again, naked! Oops! I meant 'naked' with a naked eye," replied Marve with a huge smile upon his face.

Raven chuckled under his breath.

They were standing outside the Room of Pain, the legendary training room where Valkin had first cut his teeth and locked horns with Amalgar, the steel bar.

Breakfast was served in the form of their sludge or whatever that thing was that they were given. It resembled a watered-down version of excrement that didn't quite fully solidify.

Only the weather was available to cheer them up after a meal like that. Cotton clouds puffed here & there below the great ocean-blue sky above them.

"That's not funny! And it's not going to change my mind. Naked you say! Mmm..." remarked Valkin contemplating the visage in his mind before realizing that he was just trapped into thinking those thoughts by his teachers. "Oh gosh! Ahhhhhhhh! Dammit! You guys, you're putting this crap into my head that shouldn't be there. Aw dammit, Marve! Now you see, I can't get em' out." Valkin paused for a moment and had another rethink. "Mmm! But when I think about it, it doesn't seem so bad after all. Ah! You guys. Okay, okay!" Valkin stopped his ranting and raving and composed himself to make a final decision. He took a deep breath and smiled at the death brothers who drew closer to him. "What's in it for me?" asked an intrepid Valkin. The brothers laughed and rejoiced with each other and shook Valkin's hands. They were delighted at his impending acceptance.

"The question is, are you in or out because if you're out then you're not in and if you're not in then you must be out and so there'll be nothing in it for you so really the question is, are you in?" asked Raven.

Marve had a thought he could not help but share as he tried to contain his laughter. "Hold on big brother, what if he's in and out at the same time."

"In and out is the best my brother," replied a very happy Raven as he shook hands with his younger brother also containing his laughter and the directness of the sexual insinuation.

Valkin was also about to laugh his head off as well but also remained under control and remarked, "Right, er um, I'm in but jokes aside, what's all this about really?"

"Right! So that depends entirely on you Valkin. I know this really nice place in Galapalau where you can make your move on Melody," replied Marve with a big smile on his face whilst Raven fell back a few steps to try and control his laughter. Valkin rolled his eyes with frustration and agitation.

"Come on guys, can we be serious for a moment! What's the real story here?" asked Valkin with his hands on his hips awaiting a response.

"Information little brother, information," replied Raven with a smile on his face.

Valkin shook his head now understanding the true purpose of his visit to the Sarcodian princess.

"Right, we should start preparing soon, guys. When can we leave? We should be on our way! Not a moment to lose. A woman is in distress. We should go right now!" replied a suddenly very, very eager Valkin who looked as if he had ants in his pants with all that movement.

Raven and Marve looked at each other and then at Valkin and shook their heads laughing loudly as they walked past Valkin tapping him on the shoulders and shaking their heads to meet up with the huge frame of Rufor Rafelieus coming up behind Valkin who spun around to greet the big wolf.

"RUFOR! What in the world happened to you brother!" asked an amazed Valkin to meet his once beautiful wolven friend who was now transformed into a handsome, large black stallion. Rufor bore the visage of the largest Shire horse ever constructed by the Magicians. He wore a plain brown saddle, no armor that may attract too much attention at the contest. His cloud-white muzzle ended with a pinkish tinge towards his mouth and chin groove. His forelegs were covered with an amalgamation of pearl white and overcast grey from his forearm extending to his knees covering the cannons, pasterns, ergots, and heels. A pronounced infusion of strong black and pearl white hair traveled down his hind legs covering his hock, chestnut, cannons, fetlocks, coronets, and hooves. His long tail protruded out like a majestic tuft of hair as he stood 6 ft high from the ground with bulging muscles.

Valkin approached Rufor, stroked and hugged him out of sheer sympathy caressing his brilliant, fine black hair and coat of fur.

"Please don't ask! It was Vallentor's idea of getting you into the contest. I hope you can see that sacrifices had to be made." Rufor's teary large eyes were filled with intense grief as he reeked of a scent that he was not used to.

"Oh, I can see that! Aw, Vallentor shouldn't have!" replied Valkin taking full advantage of the opportunity to mock Rufor, the Werethallic wolf king.

"Valkin, stop your bloody nonsense! You will never understand! An elite wolven king of the Werethallic army like myself reduced to a MERE PONY!" Rufor was almost in tears once again whilst everyone else was about to burst out in laughter.

Valkin jumped on top of Rufor and whispered into his twitching horse ears.

"If you are a good pony, when we get back, I'll give you an entire bale of hay. How does that sound!"

That sent Rufor into a towering fit of rage, which made him seeth with anger. He was about to kick the life out of Valkin with his hind legs when Valkin quickly changed his tune seeing that he should quickly end the joke.

"I meant rabbit cottage pie," replied Valkin quickly.

Just as the tears were about to roll down Rufor's cheek, the smell and visage of that tasty cottage pie cheered him up instantly.

The fender of the saddle bore markings that Valkin was not familiar with as he adjusted himself to the saddle.

"Let's get this over and done with Valkin! I have until midnight before I change back into my wolf form but I'm sure we'll be done well before then, right Valkin?" Rufor was looking for some reassurance from Valkin but didn't get any as Valkin smiled back at Rufor and nodded with mentioned a word.

The bold voice of Vallentor then sounded next to them.

"Oh, I doubt that very much Rufor so you better look for a quiet barn to spend the night in," replied Vallentor as he and a distinguished, more relaxed Tereartre strolled beside himself and Valkin. Vallentor wore his cream robes with golden embroidery today whilst Tereartre wore a sea green tunic with cold grey leather pants.

Valkin and Rufor respectfully greeted them.

Vallentor was holding some attire in his hand and Valkin noticed that the insignia on the attire was a replica of the markings he observed on the saddle.

"Come now Vallentor! Do you have so little faith in me? You guys have one-track minds you know, thinking that I'll sleep with this girl after the contest," replied Valkin with an air of objection in his voice.

"Actually, it is a miracle how you've managed to abstain from doing so for this long; perhaps the attempt on your life had something to do with it," replied Vallentor under his breath with a huge smile upon his face elbowing a laughing Raven next to him.

Marve was almost in tears with laughter as well.

"Vallentor, with all, due respect I heard that & it wasn't funny," protested a very irritated Valkin.

"It was for me! Ok, wake up boys. It's time to shine!"

Raven & Marve rubbed their eyes and dusted their clothes and stood with attention.

Tereartre smiled and turned towards Vallentor awaiting his orders.

Rufor, the black stallion now drew closer as well to listen in on the plan. He snorted and snuffed as a horse would do now & then as he was still getting used to the new body. Everyone was expecting a very serious plan to be laid out for them. Vallentor lifted his head. Everyone waited for him patiently and then he finally said, "Okay, let's get serious."

Everyone cleared their minds and expected a big speech from Vallentor. He readied himself and after a few moments, he said, "So, when's the wedding? Haha!" Vallentor then burst out in laughter whilst Rufor, Raven, and Marve rolled on the ground unable to control their laughter.

Valkin got angry at that point and turned away and started to walk towards the royal hut. He was about 160 ft away when Vallentor suddenly appeared in front of him from nowhere!

Valkin was astounded at the speed with which Vallentor moved, bridging a 160 ft gap in less than a second. It was unbelievable! It was impossible! No man alive he thought, could move at that speed! No man! It amazed and it frightened him.

Vallentor calmed himself down to make his point. "If you can't take a joke boy, what can you take? Don't take life too seriously. You'll miss out on all the fun. Besides, jokes can become a reality too, you never know." Vallentor smiled.

"That would mean taking the joke seriously. What does one take seriously then, life or jokes because life is no joke!"

"Oh shut up and accept my good advice boy!"

Valkin chuckled.

Valkin and Vallentor shook hands and smiled at one another whilst Vallentor contemplated the wisdom of the young man within.

"Okay Valkin, so this is your attire. It is the attire from the lands of Vanguard, in the far south past your home of Tillmandor. It is basic but effective. With it, you'll be able to handle anything that the gauntlet throws at you. The town of Vanguard is the remnant of a once mighty kingdom, inhabited by some of the greatest armor makers and blacksmiths in all the lands."

"Good king, question..." Vallentor cut Valkin off.

"Hold on Valkin, you're probably asking why this attire? Well, it's quite simple really. I'd rather those Sarcodians get suspicious about an unknown warrior from a known land than an unknown warrior from an unknown land. The chances are highly likely that their curiosity levels will be very high, especially after Tereartre's little show and that won't work in our favor!"

"Yes Vallentor, but..." Vallentor cut Valkin off again.

Valkin gave a sigh of defeat.

"You're worried about how you're going to get into the kingdom itself. Don't worry! Marve here has taken care of that aspect. He even registered you already. All you have to do is sign the attendance list and the class is in session. Remember to go easy on those fellows when you get into the second round. Make it look like you're weak so take a few shots but get in more. There's a lot of money at stake here. Tereartre and I would be very disappointed if you lose. Isn't that right Tereartre?"

Tereartre appeared from behind Valkin tapping his shoulders. Vallentor and Tereartre smiled at each other whilst Valkin had a look of confusion on his face.

"Relax! I'm just joking with you. I don't gamble. I make an honest living and don't believe in squandering money at the games..."

Everyone laughed momentarily. "...But seriously Valkin don't mess things up. There is a lot of money at stake here for the other people betting on you. Err' you wanted to ask me something?"

"Yes, I have many questions," replied Valkin finally getting his chance to speak.

"No time for questions, there's only time for one so make it good," replied Vallentor.

"If I win, why do I have to kiss this girl? Can't I..."

"No, you can't do that despite how much you want to," replied Vallentor dismissing Valkins ill intentions.

Valkin listened with a hangdog look upon his face.

"Remember the mission! You're going to extract information from her tonight and remember not the other way around. Do not reveal our plans to her under any circumstances, even if she's squeezing your…"

"Er,' No need to mention it Vallentor, what information good king?" Valkin interrupted Vallentor just before could finish his insinuating sentence.

"…Brains boy, I was going to say 'brains' boy. Information about the upcoming war, any plans for destroying us, stuff like that," replied Vallentor nodding his head making sure Valkin understood the mission.

Valkin gave a fake smile trying to hide his obvious deeper concerns about this mission and its true objectives.

"I have one more question good king, that crazy girl tried to kill me and us. Why should we try and engage her? She'll uncover me in no at the contest itself," asks a very concerned Valkin.

"It's covered, no pun intended, each participant wears a mask and doesn't reveal his identity for fear of embarrassment and harassment later on. So, the participants just wear their kingdom's colors and go through the contest. Here's your mask! This is expensive gear so take good care of it."

"I will. Let me guess, as I'm about to kiss her, I ask her quietly in which room she stays so we can have a little nightcap together, right Vallentor?"

"You're reading the game like a professional. I'm pleased. Yeah, something like that! Persuade her! Any more questions?" Everyone shook their heads. "Then let's get to it, the contest starts at noon tomorrow. We have no time to waste. This is your first solo assignment Valkin. I'm proud of you. Don't let me down," replied Vallentor with a very stern face. Then he smiled and said, "Just joking, have fun!"

Valkin wasn't sure whether to take Vallentor seriously or not. He wasn't even sure what he was supposed to do and how it was going to get done. He knew about the games but only as a spectator, never as a participant. He was nervous. Valkin slipped into his Vanguardian attire, which was a slicker black and trimmed silver color. It slithered onto his body and then firmly adhered to it with octopine suction. It looked heavy but was actually quite light and fairly strong. It was basically a long coat with secret inner pockets and weapon holders and quite cleverly designed.

Tereartre then approached Valkin and grabbed his shoulders. "Don't forget your axe, Dracoalia, and good luck young man!" Tereartre then threw the large, 300 lb axe to Valkin who caught it with ease and slipped it into his back carry pouch on Rufor's specially designed saddle. The 6 ft long unacceptium and charcoal black axe weighed down upon Rufor's weaker horse form but fortunately, his inner wolven strength picked him up and held the axe firm.

Tereartre then telepathically communicated with Valkin. "Be careful young warrior, especially of Melody! She will no doubt try to finish the job and this time, she will have the home-ground advantage. I'm not sure what Vallentor wishes to achieve by sending you on this mission but keep your wits about you Valkin. This mission is far more dangerous than you know!"

A look of concern and deep thought overcame Valkin's sweaty face but he did well to conceal himself behind Rufor for the moment.

"Be on your guard at all times and never take that mask off and never mention your real name to anyone. You must leave the family name of Kendor behind and take on a new name."

Valkin agreed with a slight nod of his head and wondered for a moment why Vallentor neglected to mention that small key piece of advice to him. Perhaps, in his jovial state of mind, it may have slipped his attention. Valkin brushed it aside and felt that the pause in his journey to Gillmanor was becoming uncomfortably longer than expected and decided to wrap up the conversation which Tereartre agreed was the best course of action.

"Thank you, Tereartre. I'd best be off."

Valkin jumped onto Rufor holding the horn of the saddle and took up the reins allowing his Vanguardian tasset to fold over the seat of the saddle.

Vallentor gave a blank look, which transformed into a deep breath that ended with the briefest of glances towards Tereartre who continued his apprehensive gaze towards the eager visage of Valkin and Rufor speeding off.

Valkin didn't have to smack the reins. They were indeed already off and moving quite fast, abnormally fast, faster than normal horses would run.

The lingering wolven foundation within the new body that Rufor found himself within gave him the speed of his former body which delighted and excited him. The black gates were nothing for Rufor Rafelieus who quickly and elegantly scaled them as he normally does in his wolf form. Although he was a brilliant black stallion now, he was happy to know that he did not lose his wolf abilities.

"The boy's first mission, I can't believe it," replied Marve with arms folded.

Vallentor saw them disappear over the gates. He turned to Raven and Marve and nodded to them.

Tereartre had his hands folded as his brilliant green hair flew across his wise face veiling him for a second.

The death brothers bowed and upon finding their wolves, climbed on and sped off.

Vallentor turned to Tereartre who was staring deep into the distance.

"What's on your mind, brother?"

Tereartre's eyes sank to the ground in contemplation of the reality awaiting them.

"The wave is coming Vallentor. I can feel it! The world will once again become a large prison ruled by one gatekeeper." Tereartre turned to face Vallentor with a look of dejection upon his face.

"Tereartre, you think too much! Let me put the bit back into your mouth and shift your focus, my dear friend. A little robin told me that the dragonmen from Razortor are launching a small-scale attack on us, this very afternoon!"

"WHAT!!!" There was a sadistic delight that came into Tereartre's eyes after Vallentor mentioned the possibility of an attack.

"It's true my friend," replied Vallentor gritting his teeth into a wide smile. Vallentor then looked up at the sun and then turned back to Tereartre. "Unfortunately, the robin also said that the target is the Pine forests. Again my dear friend this is all hearsay from what I've heard."

Tereartre's delight transformed into a deafening sternness and then finally anger. "King Braithwaite seems dead set on trying to wipe out our entire eastern shield which I have to admit is a good plan for him."

Tereartre looked behind him toward the forest's direction but did not clench his fists or grit his teeth. He just closed his eyes momentarily and then turned to Vallentor.

"How and why does she do it, may I ask?" Tereartre's mind was clearer now and so were his questions.

"As much as she wants us dead, she still hates her father for some odd reason which works to our advantage. She obviously works mostly at night to answer your question shortly. She sends a robin to us. There is a type that's a midnight black color and cannot be seen nor detected by anyone not following its flight path. Birds are a small price to pay for information these days."

"Amazing! Truly amazing, and she never gets caught?" asked a perplexed Tereartre.

"Well, it remains to be seen Tereartre. We don't know. Perhaps, she's being allowed to conduct her insidious affairs with us. Who knows? We have to rely on her hatred to provide us with accurate information but her father's one up on us. Who knows if he could be selling her dummies? Either way, we are in no position to be fussy. We have to take any information we can get and act upon it. I know you are deeply concerned about Valkin's well-being on this mission. Let me allay your fears by making my intentions extremely clear to you. Valkin needs to get close to the girl and find out more about her emotional status for us. Who knows what torture her father is putting her through? Getting married to Prince Michael is torture enough. I need to know if those robins are worth the price I paid for creating them." Vallentor was about to turn away from Tereartre when he remembered that he had more to tell him.

"Oh! By the way, I sent Raven and Marve to protect Valkin in the unlikely event that he is compromised. To answer your question, she sends it not from her window but from a tree where she feeds and holds them under the guise of treating them like pets, and the guards never suspect her, nor her hand movements. They never pick up her slight and sly mouth movements that attach the message to the songs of the bird." Tereartre thought about all of this for a few moments and showed no emotion about it.

"If what you say is true Vallentor, I will play my part and prevent them from reaching Hallucagenia Vallentor. The eastern side will not falter. You have my word," exclaimed Tereartre with a strong resolute demeanor.

"Save your strength, Tereartre. They will never get to Hallucagenia!" Vallentor walked forward towards a bow that was leaning against the table in front of them and picked it up and pulled on the string taking imaginary aim at a target. He then placed the bow down and took out a shiny object that resembled a raw crystal and smiled at it.

"What's that Vallentor?" asked Tereartre. Vallentor then turned and faced Tereartre.

"This my friend, is Perusium!"

Gillmanor, the orange and red

Kingdom

"Damn Rufor! This place is really fucking orange and red. Every second building's color is one of the two. I've heard stories of this place but never did I think it would be so excessively filled with these two colors. Not only that, look how funny the men walk, like someone, is constantly pushing them from behind but check the women out brother! They're quite beautiful, aren't they? Immaculate!"

Gillmanor was noted for its beautiful women and also for its strange choice of colors. They really did like their tangerine and cherry hues, which were the dominant colors of their insignia. The buildings, the shops, the tents, and even most of their clothes were all mixtures and variations of the two.

Valkin was beginning to wonder whether there was something wrong with these people. Have they no individuality or were they robbed of it, he thought?

"Focus Valkin, if I don't get back to the way I was by this evening, I'm going to hold you personally responsible and stomp upon your nuts until they crack. No wait! I'll teach you about some poisonous flower but lie and say it's harmless and let you get infected with the poison causing uncontrollable chronic diarrhea and flatulence, especially in the vicinity of women. How about that?" Rufor was annoyed but made light-hearted jokes to mask his frustrations. His constant whining showed it.

"Alright, alright! You've made your point ol' friend. You don't have to do that."

The two warriors were making their way through a busy alley filled with street vendors selling their goods.

People were staring at them funnily until Valkin flashed them his invitation to the gauntlet games. They then smiled, nodded, and motioned for him to continue the way he was going to the main training area where the contest was taking place.

Valkin trusted them seeing that it was the locality with the highest concentration of people.

Rufor decided that it was a good time to get an itch.

"You're lucky, only you can hear me. My bloody nose is itching and I can't scratch it. Atchuu!!!" Rufor's sinuses started to act up. "I hate being a horse! I hate being a bloody horse! I can't scratch my nose. My arse hurts! My back hurts! Valkin, just beat the shit out of these guys, talk to your woman & let's get out of this wretched place?" replied a very agitated Rufor as he shook his magnificent black coat.

Valkin laughed and scratched Rufor's nose for him. "Rufor, we can't rush things. We've got to focus on the mission and not raise too many eyebrows with our behavior."

"As if your bloody kit doesn't already attract too much attention. That's very encouraging coming from you, lover boy. Well, my mission is to get back to my old self as soon as possible. Your mission is the side mission next to this main mission, remember that," smiled Rufor.

"Stop whining. Hey! Look! We're here."

"Oh, my word! What in the world is that?" replied Rufor with a look of awe and wonder upon his horse face.

"Judging by how that poor soul just fell off the edge of that thing and probably broke all the bones in his body, I'm guessing that would be the gauntlet!"

"Hey Valkin, look! There's your damsel in distress, up there on the balcony overlooking the Colosseum. Quick! Put on the mask and let's go! It looks like the shows have already begun," cautioned Rufor as they made their way toward the gauntlet.

Valkin could easily make her out in her stunning red velvet dress that waved and cracked in the wind and of course, she was the fairest of them all. Valkin quickly slipped on his Vanguardian mask and walked towards the man who was taking the register of all the participants. Valkin honestly looked like a criminal, coming to steal money in the treasury with his silvery black mask.

The Gillmanorian man in charge of registration was short and surprisingly quite friendly seated at a quaint little desk right in front of the gauntlet. The colors of his tunic and tights were naturally imbued with hues of carrot orange and apple red. He resembled a half-ripened tomato with a chubby overhanging stomach in front of him. He sifted through all the insignia trying to find one that matched Valkin's attire. Many were still left unopened, as many participants didn't pitch for the event, out of common sense and more out of sheer fear. After finding the correct papers that matched the insignia sewn onto Valkin's attire, the registrar smiled.

"Ah! Here we are. Friedrich Stainkiller from Vanguard; Vanguard, never really heard of the land Vanguard."

"We're way down South."

"Nice! Anyway, you really must hurry now. You are the very last participant to register. I don't expect anyone else to show up today. Fortunately for you, young lad, the competition has just begun and we wouldn't want you to miss out on anything. Please sign here."

Valkin smiled under his mask and just ticked the paper.

"Excellent! You may leave your steed here. We will take him to our very classy stable shortly. Just go down this pathway, which leads to the first part of the competition, The Battle Test! You'll be given further instructions when you get there."

"Great!" replied Valkin who checked if his sword was still in his belt.

Rufor had a blank look on his face for a while which then changed into one of revenge that only Valkin could pick up.

Valkin chuckled silently and knew that he could not risk bringing Rufor along and so he walked down the gravel and stone path drenched with mud that developed from yesterday's rains, which lead to the Colosseum. When he got there, he realized why the crowd was so enthralled with the first contest. He saw a huge man who could easily pass off as a barbarian in the middle of a ring demarcated with white powder disturbed by splatters of blood and scuff marks and surrounded by choking dust and sand that clouded the air with immense tension and lack of clarity. Valkin heard loud shouts, cheers, and jests from the crowd. He saw that the man was surrounded by others warriors from all the lands; all were wearing their masks and dressed in the colors of their lands. This warrior in the middle was, no doubt, the champion, and Valkin's first challenge.

Valkin tapped one of the warrior's shoulders. He was a middle-aged man, maybe in his thirties clad in cold grey and oil black with red streaks that ran along his proud armor. He was definitely a Sarcodian knight. Valkin asked him if this was the first part of the competition.

"No mate, you actually have a choice but the question is, which method do you prefer for breaking your bones, the fucking gauntlet over there or the fat guy over here? On top of that, you have to successfully complete both challenges to kiss the fairest lady in all the lands and get the twenty thousand zafrith[2]. By the way, my name's Kendrick." Kendrick's voice was soft and crisp.

"Sounds like the odds are heavily stacked against us, Kendrick!" replied Valkin with some disappointment in his voice.

"It's designed that way, mate. You see, no one is meant to win and to date, no one has won," replied the warrior as Valkin cut in, "...but twenty thousand zafrith, wow, that's a lot of money! What a shame to let all that go?"

"It's not the money, the warriors are after mate. It's the bloody kiss! Have you seen Princess Melody mate, she's a fucking goddess that walks upon this world."

Valkin in his mind was seething with rage. He thought to himself about the circumstances of their prior meetings and how she tried to kill him and his friends! To him, she was the opposite of a Goddess. He stopped his inner escapades and refocused his attention on Kendrick's reasons.

"I'd break all my fucking bones just to get a kiss from her mate. What are you in it for mate?"

Valkin thought long and hard about his next answer figuring he shouldn't give too much away. He never really had too much to give

---

[2] Zafrith, the currency of the day

away. The more Valkin thought about it, the more it stressed him out. He shook his head and composed himself giving the most sensible answer he could think of, the same one as before.

"I'm in it for the money friend. By the way, the name's Friedrich. Friedrich Stainkiller from Vanguard." Valkin shook Kendrick's hand.

"Vanguard, does it still exist? I thought that kingdom was destroyed?"

Valkin was entirely stumped by Kendrick's assertion that his fictitious home was but a memory. He didn't know what to say. He thought that no one was supposed to know this kingdom but here's a guy who does. This is absolutely ridiculous, thought Valkin. The sweat dripped down his face and alarmed him of the need to quickly respond or get away.

"It has been rebuilt since then."

"Well, thats good news! I thought we had unfortunately destroyed it for good. Its resilience is quite admirable! I should like to visit someday and buy some swords maybe if I won the money of course. What would you do if you won the money?"

"You know Kendrick. I think I'll give it to you. Please excuse me." Valkin shook Kendrick's hand once again and departed, leaving Kendrick puzzled and dazed.

Valkin slowly made his way through the scores of cheers and shouts of warriors towards the inner ring where the champion was. Of course, every champion must have an annoying overconfident manager, and Borax the Savage, champion for seven years now since the inception of the contest, was no exception.

His manager was a short and stubby man with a greying mustache that looked like a handlebar. He wore a greasy black cap and suit with a pristine white shirt inside, no doubt, purchased from all the bets he had won. He also had a stick in his right hand, which he used to point at everyone and ridicule them.

Borax, on the other hand, was a truly savage being. Everyone who faced him, either broke a bone or lost their lives to his vicious wrath. They never came out of a fight quite the same! It was always worse than when they entered the ring with the "Beast". This nearly, 7 ft tall giant of a man had been ruthless for many years now with his hairy face & chest and large, round frame that punished many a warrior. At least, he refused to wear an orange and red mask, thought Valkin. It was such a pity that the competition was designed in such a way that no one could win it. How happy must Prince Michael feel about that, thought Valkin. Gets a kiss for doing absolutely nothing, he thought. Borax's manager shouted.

"Who has the guts to face the undefeated, undisputed champion of Gillmanor, Borax the Savage? Haha! Just as I thought, no more this year. Now you can all fuck off into your little rat holes where you belong! Borax, let's leave these losers behind. Looks like there are no real men left except maybe for that idiot who tried to take on the gauntlet, OH I BEG YOUR PARDON, WHAT'S THAT I SEE, THEY'RE TAKING HIM AWAY IN A STRETCHER! I wonder if his heart's broken too. That's what happens to the unworthy and weak, HAHAHA! What a fucking idiot!"

At that moment, about ten of the enrolled warriors forfeited and made their way back to the entrance. They decided that they weren't going to be part of another humiliating massacre. The crowd of warriors surrounding the ring became thinner and the mob was booing the defeaters as they walked back in shame to the registering table to deregister.

Borax couldn't talk. He could only scream and grunt. That's why his manager did all the talking and so, he screamed in agreement and raised his hands high in victory even though he didn't do anything.

Just as the two were about to leave the ring, a young man's voice was heard from the crowd of warriors.

"You may be right, master manager. Then, that means only a madman must accept your challenge and I have to say that I'm feeling pretty mad this morning," replied the voice.

"And who might you be, young fool or madman? SHOW YOURSELF and come forth! Please do not slip and come out fifth. HAHA!" asked the manager in a condescending, laughing tone with his thick arms comfortably folded behind his plump body.

Valkin took one step inside the ring introducing himself to everyone.

"The name's Friedrich, Friedrich Stainkiller from Vanguard. You have quite a sense of humor. So it's true, those who blow hot air tend to tell dry jokes too. Haha, very funny! I'm not in the mood for jokes master managers, so if Borats or Borcrap or whatever he's called is ready, I'd like to get this over and done with." Valkin snapped back with a bit of his humor towards a very surprised manager. He found himself on the receiving end for a change.

"Friedrich from Vanguard. I thought your lands were destroyed by Sarcodia!"

"It has been rebuilt!"

"Oh good! Pity, you won't be able to rebuild yourself after you get pummeled by Borax over here. You're right boy. You must be mad to even show up here! Mad, not brave!"

"You know master manager…" replied Valkin as he entered the ring and faced the old man, "…you've taught me something today."

"And what's that Friedrich from Vanguard?" replied the manager with his nose all flared up in defense.

"Never listen to the comments of someone who doesn't know you."

The manager was taken aback by the apparent lack of respect by this newcomer warrior.

"HOW DARE YOU INSULT ME! I'd say, boy! You'd better watch your watch because the show is about, to begin with, your end, boy."

Borax's manager sized Valkin up with a condescending eye and then walked up to Borax and whispered to him before turning his attention back to Valkin. "Friedrich!! What kind of a name is that? It's very weak!"

Valkin did not reply.

Borax's manager whispered into his ear once again. "The lad's cocky and stupid! I've seen them come and go. Make an example of him. Don't hold back."

Borax roared and then without warning, he ran straight toward Valkin at full speed.

Valkin saw him coming and simply jumped to his right whilst putting his leg out effectively tripping the giant.

Borax hit the ground hard and headfirst and slid almost to the very edge of the circle. Now, Valkin was tall but not as tall as the giant Borax so when Borax stood up again, then only did Valkin realize how short he really was.

The news of the fight was spreading fast and it reached the royalty on the balcony in no time causing them to turn their attention to the battle ring because some crazy guy was stupid enough to take on Borax, the Savage. From the royal balcony, everyone could see the fight including

Princess Melody who suddenly became curious as to who this fighter was.

The fight was on!

Borax dusted himself and was becoming very, very angry. He stood tall and slowly turned his vibrating head towards Valkin who was standing normally with his arms at his sides. Borax started a slow jog towards Valkin.

Valkin also started a slow jog towards Borax. The two clashed with each other, each holding his ground. Neither was willing to back down nor give up his position. They were locked in a body-breaking bear hug.

Everyone was shocked but the most surprised was Borax's manager. Up until now, no one had ever managed to hold Borax stationary like that. He was nervous, very nervous!

Borax was growling like a mad Bararg enraged with fury and revenge, whilst Valkin gritted his teeth as he remembered all that was taught to him by his masters about strength.

Valkin didn't feel fatigued at all. He was quite alright. He didn't even break a sweat! He then decided to test the limits of his strength by giving Borax a taste of his own medicine. He suddenly pushed Borax backward and jumped up as he did. As Borax was unnaturally taller than him he gave him a left hook that surprised and dazed the giant a little sending him staggering backward waving his arms in the air to maintain his sense of balance. Valkin then followed it up with a right and then another left that was delivered almost instantaneously. Each blow was thunderous sending shockwaves throughout the crowds that began to gather around to witness the spectacle.

Borax's manager's jaw dropped and a look of horror befell his cheeky face.

Valkin decided to finish Borax off with a jumping elbow-shot to the head, which further dazed the giant but still couldn't bring him to the ground.

Borax had no reply to Valkin's vicious onslaught. It was at that point in the fight that he was struggling to see.

Valkin was tempted to slice him but that would breach the rules of the contest and even worse, it would breach Bruce's rules of engagement and then Valkin would have to forfeit. Valkin didn't want that. He knew that the fight would soon be over. To his surprise, Borax quickly recovered and had a look of death upon his face. He started an ominous run towards Valkin, who momentarily found himself paralyzed with unnecessary fear instilled in him by the approaching giant.

Borax met Valkin halfway spearing him hard into the ground. Valkin hit the ground back-first with a large thud that shook the earth letting out a deafening scream of pain that shocked the crowd who was cheering for him making them bellow out a collective sigh of sympathy fearing that the young challenger's brave stand was alas, at an end. The wind was knocked out of Valkin's aching chest for a moment.

Borax got up from the ground, smiled, and then roared to the crowd.

Valkin blinked his eyes and tried to feel any for broken bones in his body but was quite surprised to feel none. After the initial shock of pain, he felt, he was now back to normal. He smiled as he lied on the ground watching clouds pass by blue skies of sunshine. He enjoyed the moment. He never felt this way before. He felt really good! Without Borax knowing it, Valkin nipped up from the ground and started to run toward him. He jumped on top of Borax's back and caught him in a choke hold. A shocked Borax then went on a mad rampage to free himself from the clutches of Valkin, the overgrown flea that latched onto his back. Borax tried to do everything to get out of it but failed. Eventually, Valkin's grip brought him down to one knee as the air slowly diminished in Borax's large chest and then eventually Valkin brought Borax down to both knees as the crowd cheered Valkin on.

The manager couldn't believe his eyes and the worst part was that he couldn't interfere, partly because he wouldn't know how to. They never lost a fight before and it was against the rules for him to interfere. Borax himself didn't realize that Valkin was this strong. All the weight training that Valkin did was paying off. It took almost a quarter of an hour for the giant to eventually pass out; then only did Valkin release his vice-like grip upon him. The interesting aspect for Valkin was that he was using only a tiny fraction of his strength. That's how he felt! Valkin himself also held back his true strength for good reasons.

Close by, two warriors clad in secretive black cloaks were closely watching the fight from the crowd and then left shortly after Valkin defeated Borax.

The manager was so deeply disappointed about the humiliating defeat that he was too reluctant to approach Valkin afterward. However, those feelings then slowly transformed into humility and appreciation of this nineteen-year-old boy; so much so, that he took off his hat and went over to Valkin standing in the middle of the ring, and shook his hand.

"I have nothing to say, boy, except that you have taught me a valuable lesson today. You have earned the right to proceed to the next stage of the contest. I wish you all the best!"

Valkin smiled and bowed to the manager and lifted his hands to the crowds waving to them and acknowledging their unwavering support.

Finally, the deadly gauntlet which had broken many warriors before lay before the advancing figure of Valkin. It was a 30 ft tall structure consisting of rotating platforms, chopping axes, and slicing blades that swung back and forth waiting for an opportunity to slice and dice anyone stupid enough to step forth upon it. No-one had ever made it to the third stage of blades. They always got clobbered off at the second stage hitting the ground hard never to return for a second attempt.

Valkin walked up to the structure situated just behind the fighting ring and gazed upwards examining its length and breadth. He took a deep breath. Then, he ascended the great ladder to the beginning platform of the gauntlet. His dark purple and jet-black cloak was blowing in the wind. He felt that it would hinder him in this challenge so he discarded it leaving only a thin long sleeve black tunic to protect him.

Elsewhere, somehow, Rufor got out of the stables by rendering the guards unconscious with two hard kicks to their heads. He pushed through the angry crowds and made his way to a good spot where he could catch all the action. Any guards that tried to subdue him were simply laid out by his powerful kicks. Fortunately, his height was a great advantage as his towering figure allowed him to catch all the action.

The news of the epic defeat of Borax captured the royals' attention, especially that of Melody who was becoming very curious as to who this mystery warrior was. Valkin rubbed his hands with chalk and ran towards the gauntlet. He looked up the ladder, took a deep breath, and started to climb. He reached the top of the structure only after a few minutes where a Gillmanorian man was waiting to receive him.

The man was masked as well and was holding protective gear made from leather and hippo hide, which relieved Valkin very much. The man passed Valkin the gear and simply said, "You're going to need it, boy!"

Both Valkin and the man passed a somber stare towards each other under their masks, which concealed their true identities as well as their feelings.

As Valkin was about to start his first attempt the man said to him, "Good luck son! I don't like my job because it involves making things harder for you. That's why I am saying now in the outset, please forgive me when I do eventually make things harder for you."

"Well sir, don't worry about it. I like a good challenge. Thanks, old man for telling me though; I appreciate it."

Valkin, now all clad with his gear was all set, ready to go. He glanced up at the royal balcony with determined deep brown hazel eyes. The image he saw was of Princess Melody. It was a short glance but she saw him as well, staring at her, as if to say, "I'm coming to get you!" She felt a nostalgic feeling well up in her bosom. Her woman intuition kicked in telling her that she met this person somewhere before but she eventually shrugged off the thought, feeling that such a thing was impossible. A look of despair befell her face once again. It was a look she disguised very well, a look that only her father could detect and be concerned about.

Valkin then faced forward to focus on the task that lay before him. The gauntlet was the ultimate challenge for any warrior considering the kiss or the prize money. The trick was to survive the 30 ft structure of death.

"One, two, one, two, three!" counted Valkin in his mind. Valkin stepped on the rotating platform and found it very difficult to stand upon and so he crouched low before he lost his balance risking being flung completely off. The speed that the platform was rotating seemed to increase when an individual stood upon it or so it seemed. The wooden platform was rotating anticlockwise and something else was rotating with it! Just above were stabbing knives that were coming down just above Valkin's head lashing out to lop off his head. If he stood up, he would get cut severely by the saw-like action of those knives. Valkin could only get glances at the second stage, which seemed even more impossible to get through. The clubs swung from left to right but not in perfect synch. They were just slightly off-synch, which didn't help much anyway. Also, Valkin couldn't make out the distance between each club from where he was and surmised the reason why his predecessor got flung off. Valkin didn't want to focus too much on the last stage with blades of death but he did see two vitally important things within the gauntlet. There were only two breakpoints in the gauntlet; one was the first stage itself and the second was a narrow plank, only a foot in breadth, connecting the second and third stages which were what Valkin was looking for. He also figured that the trick to the gauntlet was speed without hesitation. Now, the only place he knew he'd have to hesitate was on that 1 ft plank because he would need time to figure out how to complete the third stage. For now, he thought he'd take a breather back at the start.

The crowd that was about to erupt in cheers a moment ago thinking Valkin was going to go for it now began ridiculing and booing Valkin who rejoined the old man back at the start. Valkin smiled at him, rubbed his hands, loosened his neck getting ready for liftoff.

"What's wrong boy? Had a change of heart?" asked the old man with frizzy white hair and a big smile under his mask.

"No, just a change of mind."

The old man did not understand what Valkin meant by his words. He mistook Valkin's strategizing for bailing on the event, a misinterpretation that he was about to discover to the true extent.

At that declaration and to everyone's surprise, Valkin leaped onto the rotating platform again and the crowd went wild! He rolled over to his right allowing the rotation to bring him within proximity to the next stage but he had to time his jump or else suffer getting severely clobbered by the swinging primate clubs. His jump was perfect as he rolled on his back and landed in between the second and third clubs. He was very lucky! If those clubs were any closer to each other, he would have been smacked by both of them solidly! The pendulum-like motion of the clubs and the deliberately designed synchronicity of their swing made it very difficult for Valkin to maneuver. He knew he couldn't hold his position for long and so he decided to make another jump for it. He waited until the third club was just outside his forward gaze and then jumped forward and repeated his roll but this time he jumped forward to reach the plank and was clipped by the fifth and final club!

The crowd gave a collective sigh of horror thinking that this was it but when they saw that he was fine, they cheered loudly.

The club hit the outside of his calf muscle but it wasn't too serious. However, it was only until he got a good look at the last stage that he regretted ever taking part in the gauntlet in the first place. The blades of the "death stage" as it was called were powered by a complicated gear and pulley system that allowed the blades to rotate and stab outwards in random directions. There were three sets of three blades. They were alternating and very difficult, if not impossible to overcome. The directions of stabbing for the three sets of blades were different for each set. Valkin had to think fast but he knew he had a couple of minutes to think and gather himself on that narrow plank so he took his time. Little did Valkin realize that Prince Michael, "the ass" gave a signal to the old man who designed and built the gauntlet to move the clubs forward to speed up Valkin's downfall. Valkin didn't realize it until he heard an unhealthy lever sounding behind him and he knew that something sinister was up. He could feel it and sensed that he was in trouble; so he decided to put it all on the line and move forward! Luckily, he did because the clubs started to inch their way forward toward him right after he jumped. Valkin didn't receive any combat training from Raven or Marve. They just simply improved his strength and his speed. Bruce, however, showed him how to wield and dodge weapons of all shapes and sizes. Bruce emphasized that the warrior did not only use his eyesight but engaged all of his senses in combat. The warrior feels, hears, and senses the movements of his adversary and strikes with deadly accuracy and efficiency. Valkin could feel the clubs creeping up behind him and the sweat dripping down the side of his face. The sudden heaviness of his gear weighed him down as the shouts and screams of the crowd deafened him. Valkin closed his eyes and gathered his thoughts and concentration. Then, he remembered what Bruce told him about being there and not being there and how to block out everything else but the target. Valkin then opened his eyes and jumped forward just missing the deadly swing of the clubs behind him. A blade shot out from the wooden floor as he jumped up to hold the top planks of the wooden structure. Two then shot out from the sides, one after the other twirling and whistling in the air. Valkin quickly pulled himself up as they did and jumped to the space in between the first and second set. Blades from the second set were on him now. This time, their attack pattern was diagonal and aimed at Valkin's groin.

"Oh No! Not the precious goods!" exclaimed Valkin as he just managed to dodge the blade. The bottom blade shot out but Valkin somehow sensed that the next two blades were going to shoot out together soon after. So he side-stepped the first and quickly pulled his hands into his protective sleeves, jumped, and grabbed the two blades stretching his head backward and keeping his body off the ground. He used the momentum to jump to the second space and tackle the last set, which up until now was set in its circular slashing motion but suddenly shifted to random motions.

The controllers down below were probably given the order to make it so.

Valkin tried to find a pattern but found none!

Princess Melody and the royals were tremendously impressed at the warrior's courage thus far but somehow knew that his end was near.

Valkin conceded that he would find no pattern and took a deep breath and went for it. He dodged the first attack by the first blade from beneath and the second from the side but the third blade from the left struck him in the left arm. Luckily, his protective gear was holding true but now the blades were changing position and Valkin had to change with them quickly. Their attacks were mainly frontal ones aimed at driving Valkin back to the other sets but Valkin had enough. He ripped out his gear and gained an agility advantage, which he employed. It was at that point that he saw a loose piece of wood above about to give up and fall to its doom. He observed it and just his luck, it fell and he kicked it towards one of the blades. It stabbed it savagely giving him a window of opportunity to evade the other two. He jumped forward and rolled to the end of what seemed like a neverending competition.

Everyone put their hearts back into their chests including Princess Melody. There was a deafening wave of silence that spread among the crowd. The ladies could not believe what they had just witnessed. History was just made before their very eyes! The crowd stood up from their seats. Thousands of blank stares blanketed the silence with an air of humility. Then, they went completely beserk.

However, the look on Prince Michael's face was priceless as he sat cross-legged leaning on his hands, shaking his head. Then, he slowly, reluctantly got up suddenly as if he realized something very important and started to smile a sinister smile. He turned to his father to share his thoughts.

"Father, tell me something, is it not against the rules for any participant to damage or use any part of the structure while trying to complete the gauntlet? This Friedrich guy did damage it and that's what gave him the advantage."

King Gilleus stroked his beak-shaped beard and shook his head in disagreement with his son.

"No!" he replied with a straight face.

Prince Michael wasn't pleased, not one bit.

"Two problems son. Firstly, the gauntlet and this entire competition have no rules, so anything goes. More than that, it was designed so that no-one was ever supposed to win. Now, if I or you suddenly say that this young warrior has done something that wasn't in the rulebook then our good people will ask 'what rulebook, we never heard of any rulebook!' This will lead to various holes in our credibility by such disingenuous behavior but relax son; I don't expect you to understand the complexities of the political landscape just yet."

"I understand very well father. You'd rather humiliate me, your son than compromise your good standing with Gillmanor," replied Prince Michael as he got up from his throne.

King Gilleus smiled with satisfaction upon his wise face.

Princess Melody who was seated next to Prince Michael was listening to the entire conversation and pretended she didn't hear anything but giggled on the inside.

"I didn't say that, son. I only implied that politics is an area of development for you son. Look, what's a single kiss compared to a lifetime of kisses? Cheer up, son. The outcome is not as bad as you think it is," replied King Gilleus as he stood up and tapped his son's shoulder trying to comfort him.

"The crowd is waiting for you. Get into their good books and show them what a good king you can be one day."

"Still, like you said father, it was designed so that no-one was ever supposed to win. Nonetheless, Thank you father for your advice," replied Prince Michael with a noticeable tinge of disappointment upon his face.

Valkin was still on the end platform and enjoying every moment of his impossible victory. He was jumping up and down, blowing kisses to all the ladies in the crowd! The people from the colosseum stands could not be contained and overcame the few guards that were stationed there for crowd control. They ran up to the gauntlet and threw beautiful carnations at Valkin. He caught one, kissed it, and threw it back. The women were going wild and Valkin was milking every bit of it. He felt like a superhero with that mask on. His anonymity was liberating! He knew that today he made history and no-one was going to change that.

The other participants were initially shocked and struck with awe at what they had just witnessed.

King Braithwaite just sat quietly through it all with his son Prince Bartholomew standing behind him. They watched the event unfold with his keen eyes. He never uttered a word. He sat next to the beautiful Queen Alekto with his hands folded wearing a wry, snug smile.

Prince Michael was annoyed and frustrated and wanted to hurry up the proceedings so he motioned for the winner to come to the balcony.

Valkin saw him and so he slid down the side of the gauntlet along a plank. By the time he had reached the ground, enough guards were on the scene to shield his ascent up the stairs leading to the balcony. The guards had to control quite a number of ladies who were trying to grab onto Valkin and kiss him. The inundation of so many women at one time was overwhelming for Valkin. He really appreciated it. He made his way up the stairs, feeling quite chaffed with himself, and to the top of the balcony where all the royals were seated. He went up the left stairs leading to the top so he could greet Princess Melody first and then the other royal members. As Valkin ascended the stone stairs, the visage of Princess Melody erupted into a volcanic explosion of cherry red and stripes of tiger orange that overflowed towards Valkin completely consuming his former thoughts and dispatching the beautiful Princess.

She eagerly awaited the arrival of the knight in dull armor who conquered the Gauntlet to claim a kiss from the Princess or the money. She wasn't sure which order was preferable for the warrior.

Valkin ascended with his slick black and trimmed silver-colored Vanguardian regalia which impressed Princess Melody greatly. He approached her slowly. She looked absolutely ravishing in her red volcanic ash dress. They finally met after many days of loneliness that they were completely unaware of. Valkin held her hand for an eternity and bowed. She bowed as well and smiled at the masked warrior.

Everyone else was seated overlooking the crowds.

Prince Michael was standing with a look of intense irritation on his face as Valkin bowed to his prospective wife.

"My lady..." replied Valkin in the softest, unsuspecting voice he could muster.

"Ur' em', congratulations Friedrich, you have surprised us all," replied a very annoyed Prince Micheal.

"Hope it wasn't too much of a surprise," replied Valkin as he shifted to greet Prince Micheal.

The crease in Melody's eyebrows was priceless as she slowly turned her head towards the masked warrior now knowing that she had heard his voice before.

Valkin couldn't help it. His excitement was too great and so he bowed and also hugged Prince Michael who was not used to being hugged by normal men.

"Prince Michael, I just want to say, thank you for this opportunity." Valkin then bowed down to King Gilleus and King Braithwaite who nodded their heads in recognition and he finally waved to Queen Alekto who smiled in return.

Prince Michael swallowed hard and then walked forward to address the people of Gillmanor who became quiet only after a few minutes as he approached the edge of the balcony.

"Citizens of Gillmanor! Citizens of Sarcodia! And to all others who have joined us to witness this truly magnificent spectacle. I present to you, your champion, Friedrich Stainkiller of Vanguard!" Prince Michael pointed to Valkin who walked forward and waved to the crowd and then bowed to them.

The people went crazy and erupted into vociferous applause!

Prince Michael rolled his eyes upwards as he half-heartedly clapped his hands with no real conviction.

Valkin then pointed to his girl fan club below motioning with his lips that he did it just for them.

Princess Melody's nose automatically twitched for a second as she looked away trying not to notice Valkin's flirting. She couldn't explain it, but it happened and it kind of annoyed her that she found herself reacting in this manner.

Prince Michael then told Valkin to join him further back with Princess Melody and the others. Prince Michael snapped his fingers and a servant came to him holding a very solid-looking leather bag. He took it from the servant and gave it to Valkin. "Twenty thousand zafrith, as was promised!"

"Thank you, good Prince. You're very kind." Valkin took the bag and slung it across his shoulders and then proceeded to walk away towards the stairs, an act that Prince Michael found to be strange but did not hinder.

The crowd cheered and then went silent.

"Er, hurm! Friedrich!" called Prince Michael.

Valkin spun around. "Yes sir?"

Valkin waited patiently. Prince Michael had thought he'd forgotten.

"And, as promised, a kiss from my lovely wife-to-be, Princess Melody."

Valkin smiled a great big smile as he approached Princess Melody who stood up to receive his taller figure staring down at her.

Prince Micheal, however, suddenly remembered that he wanted to know what this masked warrior looked like and made his wish known to Valkin before Valkin accepted his kiss gift from Princess Melody.

"Don't you wish to remove your mask, Friedrich? It will be a lot easier to kiss your prize," asked Prince Michael with a sick look on his face.

"It'll be my pleasure," answered Valkin not realizing the implications of what he had just said, and without thinking, he removed his mask revealing his face to one and all.

Melody had her hands intertwined behind her back and was so nervous that she started to shake. As Valkin removed his mask, she could not believe her eyes.

Valkin was all sweaty and had a sooty appearance. She couldn't believe it was really him. Strangely, she felt a glimmer of hope light up within her heart that sparked a fire of defiance. Her mind went back to that day when she tried to assassinate King Vallentor along with Valkin and she felt very guilty and embarrassed to see the man she tried to kill before her.

King Braithwaite watched on, saying nothing. Only he noticed the light in his daughter's eyes. He noticed other things as well, like the resemblance this man bore to an old friend and enemy within the depths of his mind.

King Gilleus on the other seat was keeping a close eye on his long-time friend and ally, King Braithwaite. He too sensed something was amiss.

Valkin slowly approached her. He knew he had her exactly where he wanted her because he knew she couldn't do a damn thing to him, not in front of the royalty! Princess Melody felt a small trickle of sweat run down her face as Valkin tilted his head and drew his lips closer to hers holding her cheek with his left index finger.

The sudden prick that Princess Melody felt in her exposed left shoulder was numbing but not painful at all. She immediately felt drowsy as her beautiful illustrious amber eyes started to drift and close. Then, she fell into Valkin's arms before her sweet rose lips could meet his. Queen Alekto let out a shrill scream as King Braithwaite jumped out of his throne running to his daughter's aid.

"MELLY!" shouted a panic-stricken King Braithwaite. He was beside her in no time although the distance from where she stood and where he sat was some 16 ft away.

Valkin noticed the King's speed and although it was a short distance, it was still very quick, quick than normal! Valkin then seemed to take charge and direct orders.

"Quick, your highnesses into the chambers, NOW! Your guards will protect our escape." Just as Valkin uttered those cautionary remarks, an arrow pierced the skull of a guard that was protecting King Braithwaite. If that guard wasn't there, King Braithwaite surely would have been a dead man. However, King Gilleus saw what really happened. King Braithwaite grabbed a guard and used him as a shield for his protection and all of it was done in a matter of a few seconds. The Sarcodian King then turned around and focused his eyes on the crowd and saw someone run off immediately wearing a dark black cloak from a good vantage point where such a shot could have been fired. The person that ran off was almost a mile away and he could see him clearly with his hawk-like eyes and identified him immediately.

"QUICK, CALL THE DOCTOR!" shouted Prince Michael as they laid Princess Melody on the bed inside the chamber. The chamber was dark and misty now that the guards closed all the doors and windows. It was beginning to get stuffy. Being a very warm day that also didn't help at all.

Valkin pulled out the dart that was stuck in her shoulder and said, "She's burning up. Open the windows at the back and guard them with your lives guards. TOWELS AND COLD WATER PLEASE!" Valkin was calling all the shots.

Queen Alekto quickly got the towels from the royal cupboard and a bowel of water frantically in no time as the Kings looked on at the unconscious Princess with great concern.

King Braithwaite was quiet but very calm though. He was not the kind of man to panic easily. He knew exactly what Valkin was doing and allowed him to continue trusting him with the life of his daughter.

"Here, the doctor has arrived," replied King Gilleus.

The doctor came in with his toolkit and white robes. He looked more like an old healer just about to die himself. He was old and white and almost senile. He needed help and luckily, Valkin was there. The doctor slowly sat down next to Princess Melody who was now slowly drifting into a heavy slumber and examined her heart beat and kept on mumbling, "Yes! Yes!" to himself as if he knew exactly what was wrong with her. He checked her wound and nodded his head. King Braithwaite couldn't take it any longer, "Doctor, how is she? Is she going to make it?"

The doctor stood up slowly, one leg at a time, "Yes! Yes!"
"Oh thank the Gods," replied a very relieved King Braithwaite. Everyone exhaled except Valkin and King Braithwaite. He felt that Melody's life was still in danger. He felt that he should tell the doctor and hoped he believed him.

"Doctor, I don't think we're not out of the woods yet." Everyone turned to Valkin expecting an explanation which followed soon after with foreboding implications. "Smell this dart. It was laden with a fasting-acting poison."

"Let me smell it boy," requested King Braithwaite. Braithwaite smelled it and agreed. Braithwaite knew exactly what kind of poison it was and where it came from and it angered him but he remained quiet about it for now. "The boy is right. It is poison. What can we do about it?" asked King Braithwaite.

"It's a sleeping poison. I learned about it in my youth in Vanguard. It cripples its victim through a deep slumber which progresses into a coma and then eventual death."

Braithwaite agreed for he too knew about its effects very well. He knew slightly more than Valkin. He knew the plant from which the poison was made, the Iriseae[3] plant. It is indigenous to only one region in all the lands, DALLAVEGA[4], a city of power and death.

---

[3] The sleeping plant as it is known.
[4] Dallavega named after the family that rules its lands. It is called the city of power and death which speaks for itself.

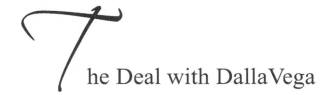

The Deal with DallaVega

Donavan DallaVega, "the Don", ruler of a DallaVega, a city half the size of Sarcodia but just as ferocious if not worse. The DallaVegan family had survived for almost seven generations now. They had seen many wars in their lifetimes and still endured. They were not part of any great Barbarian war but featured extensively in many smaller, "disputes". They do only what they feel is right for them and don't take orders from any kingdom. Their strength lies is in their vast resources, money, and something else! They are an extremely wealthy nation of people controlling most of the zafrith that flowed through the lands. No-one lives in poverty here. This is because the DallaVegan city is sitting on a vast Perusium[5] deposit. Perusium is also used to make zafrith. Perusium is an amazing substance. The bombs that can be made from this metal have the potential to blast anything from within a two to five-mile radius. This is why other kingdoms are very reluctant to take on the DallaVegans.

---

[5] Perusium, a precious metal used mainly for money generating, jewelry and also for making unstable bombs. Perusium is very rare and is a self-renewable natural resource.

"Gilleus, get Bellorus and meet me in your chambers, NOW!" requested King Braithwaite. Gilleus rushed out to find King Bellorus.

A guard then approached Valkin. "Er' Friedrich sir, your horse is acting rather unruly sir. Would you please kindly go tend to it, sir?" requested one of the guards.

"Aw geez, he could have picked a better time!" exclaimed Valkin with some disappointment. "Sure," he replied as he turned around to face everyone. "I shall return good royals." Valkin bowed feeling a bit embarrassed and ran off.

He made it to the stables in no time.

"What in the world are you doing, Rufor? Are you trying to uncover me here? I was practically in the royal's bedroom when you started to act up. What's the matter!" shouted a very angry Valkin.

"Sorry to break up the party! I needed to get your attention somehow. Look Valkin, the situation has changed and we were just ordered to pull out..." Rufor was cut off by a guard that walked by with a peculiar look on his face as he gazed at Valkin who looked as if he was having a conversation with a horse, which he was. Rufor continued, "...Keep stroking my fur and listen closely..." Valkin acknowledged and stroked the shit out of Rufor's fur. "...Listen here, we've been ordered to regroup by Raven and Marve. They're here. You've had enough fun for one day. You got to see your 'girlfriend'. Now, let's go before you attract any more attention to yourself. Vallentor wants you to begin your training immediately in the Galapalau islands." Rufor had a look of seriousness upon equine visage.

"I understand Rufor but I haven't even got in yet and why would he send me here only to call me back? Princess Melody is in a bad way and their idiot of a doctor almost sent her to her resting place through sheer negligence. Look, she got shot!

"What! Is that why she fell? Mmm...interesting."

"I know and Braithwaite seems to know who did it. Look, Ruf, I've to do something."

Rufor put his head down to think about Valkin's request.

"Look, give me some time. I'll be in and out of there, I promise. I'll stay with him and get the information we need."

"Mmm...Sorry, Val! We came here to gather information not solve a murder mystery. It's not our problem! Argh! You making things so damn hard for me." Rufor could see the concern and look of determination in Valkin's eyes and despite his best intentions to follow orders, he started to yield to Valkin's wishes. "Vallentor is not going to like this. Ok! Just remember, focus on the mission." Rufor was indecisive for a moment and then he finally yielded to Valkin's request. "You have your time Val. It should take you less than no time given to counteract the poison. Hey Valkin, they don't invite strangers to secret meetings, you know that, and if you get caught, I can't help you in this form so don't get cocky and do something unintelligent. I'll be waiting for you!"

"Hey Rufor, you have excellent hearing and you're a hard and insensitive wolf to please."

"Yah! Well, I hope you remember that if you try anything. Get out of here you little bastard!"

"Language Rufor! Haha! Understood! There's one more thing I have to do first, though."

Valkin ran to the registration man and asked where he could find Kendrick. The man told him that he could be among the other participants over at the stables. Valkin ran over to the stables and found only nine men standing there discussing the turn of events. Kendrick was nowhere to be found! Valkin started to wonder why he would leave, if he stood a chance of getting twenty thousand zafrith for free, unless, he didn't need it and just had to leave. Then, a thought ran through Valkin's mind and he suddenly changed his focus. He looked around and spoke to a man from Razortor who was close by. His cloak was fiery red and black and seemed pleasant enough to talk to. Valkin approached him and tapped him on the shoulder.

"Excuse sir, Have you seen a participant by the name of Kendrick?"

"He took off in a hurry. Said he had some stuff to take care of back home." Valkin pondered for a second and then thanked the man and made off in a hurry.

Time to go

"Friedrich, we cannot thank you enough. When my daughter awakens, I will tell her you have saved her life. Are you sure you don't want to join us for supper?" It was difficult to tell whether King Braithwaite was being polite or not. He hid his emotions and intentions so well behind a placid smile on his face. He was leaning against the great walls next to the great entrance gates with one arm.

Valkin was on his way. He could only take so much of orange & red unless they were the colors of the hazy afternoon sky, which quite thankfully it was.

King Gilleus & Prince Michael had their hands behind their backs. Princess Melody and Queen Alekto were back in the castle. The Queen opted to look after Melody.

"No, thank you, good king, for your generosity. This money will come in handy for my mother. Vanguard is many miles from here and I must get an early start if I'm to reach home before dark." Valkin was still dressed in the Vanguard attire. His mask was off though.

"It must be really difficult for you to travel with so many unruly characters about like those nasty Hallucens and DallaVegans?"

Valkin knew all about the Hallucens but nothing about the DallaVegans. Nobody mentioned anything about them to him. Valkin had a casual look on his face trying to conceal the feelings about what Braithwaite was implying. Either way, he decided to agree for the time being.

"Yes indeed the northern road is a dangerous one, but I prefer to take the Southern road, with less ruckus it's much safer. Well, look at that! The hazy sun dips into the horizon and that means that I must get going. Thank you once again for your hospitality. Take care and may we meet again."

"One moment Friedrich…" said King Braithwaite as he drew King Gilleus's sword from his belt. King Gilleus was taken aback by Braithwaite's apparent and sudden urge to fight and so was Valkin. Rufor didn't like it one bit and time was running out.

Prince Michael waited in anticipation of a fight with a smile on his ugly face.

"Good King, have I offended you in some way?" asked Valkin with his hands up in a gesture of peace. His axe was slung across his back and his sword was hidden under his coat.

"Not in the least Friedrich. I just felt like having a friendly bout with you, to say, I fought with the champion."

"I would love to but I am so sorry my good king. My body aches and the long journey home awaits me. And besides, it would be unwise & foolish of me to take on the great King of Sarcodia, such class cannot compare with the level of skill and requires another occasion to grace, if the King permits such a suggestion?"

"Fair enough lad! Good luck on your journey! I will wait for your return to fight you. Until then, farewell! May you be kept safe."

Then without warning, King Braithwaite swung the sword at Valkin's torso with the intention of cleaving him in half but found his sword stopped by Valkin's large axe.

Valkin gritted his teeth as he held onto the axe with literally all his might. The blow was so strong it eventually brought him down to one knee.

King Braithwaite held him there with just his one hand and eventually threw the sword back to a very intrigued King Gilleus who caught it by the handle and sheathed it.

The royal guard escort was also intrigued at their King's gesture and wondered what that was all about!

King Gilleus looked down upon Valkin and smiled.

Valkin smiled back and got up to his feet.

"Please forgive me. I was just checking to see if you can handle yourself. It would seem that you can," remarked King Braithwaite with a look of relief upon his face.

Valkin nodded in acknowledgment. "Thank you, good king." Valkin then mounted his trusty steed, Rufor, and sped off toward the direction of Sarcodia with haste.

King Gilleus was intrigued and wanted an explanation from King Braithwaite. "What is it, Braithwaite? What was all that about just now with the boy?" asked Gilleus as he approached King Braithwaite from behind.

"That boy, Gilleus, is a Hallucen!"

"WHAAT! How can you be sure? " asked Prince Michael with a look of shock and dismay upon his weak and thin face as he felt a tremor travel down his timid, weak body when the word 'Hallucen' was mentioned.

"The markings on his axe," replied an emotionless stone-faced King Braithwaite. King Gilleus moved in front of Braithwaite to confront him on this accusation.

"Hold on. There weren't any markings on his axe as far as I saw," replied Prince Michael in the background.

King Gilleus gave up his pretense and began to laugh.

"There were, you just did not see it, young Prince. I was wondering when you were going to confirm Braithwaite. They were finely engraved and barely visible to the naked eye. I know those markings. I've seen them before. The work of Bryce is unmistakable! I'll get my finest men to follow him and give me a full report within the day. They'll take care of him, quickly and cleanly if you wish."

"Haha! No, No! Let the boy go!" replied King Braithwaite with a noticeable increase in the volume of his voice. "Vallentor has plans for him, so he must follow through. The time is drawing nearer for my interference but for now, I must remain a quiet observer. I see that Raven hasn't lost his touch either. Interesting, very interesting!" replied King Braithwaite rubbing his hairy chin.

King Gilleus smiled whilst Prince Michael looked completely baffled. He was out of the conversation from the very beginning.

"Let Vallentor do his thing, Gilleus. My curiosity exceeds my rage for the moment. I'm not sure how I will feel tomorrow!"

"You really don't know what he's got up his sleeve, do you, Braithwaite?" King Braithwaite laughed and turned around to face the solemn face of King Gilleus.

"No, I don't! Do what you must Gilleus. This is our first opportunity since my daughter returned. The faint trickle of sweat that ran down her neck when this Friedrich man was about to kiss her could only mean that it was someone she remotely has feelings for. A savior perhaps, to rescue her from her predicament. Someone within the Hallucen ranks that she had met and decided to kill but failed to do so. Bellorus and the legion retrieved her when she failed to assassinate the top-level structure of Hallucagenia to put into motion the secondary part of the plan which was bold, granted, but very insightful!" King Braithwaite smiled with realization in his resolute cedar dark brown eyes. "I threw the Hallucens a bone, and they took the bait. Guess what! Now we know who we are dealing with, Gilleus." King Braithwaite turned to face his colleague, King Gilleus with the development of a red sunset in his eyes. "That was Valkin Kendor Gilleus, son of Helleus Kendor, my sworn enemy."

"What!" King Gilleus had a look of confusion and wonder trying to connect the memories he had of Helleus Kendor with that of Valkin's face and the more he thought about it, the more closely Valkin resembled Helleus.

"Yes, it is true! However, I have my own plans, which I will follow through with."

King Gilleus smiled, bowed, and retreated to the royal chambers.

Prince Michael followed looking back at King Braithwaite constantly with awe and horror.

King Braithwaite stayed behind and observed the hazy orange sky with a look of sadness mixed with bliss in his own jaded eyes.

$\mathcal{B}$ ellorus's Breakthrough

"My lord, I have received wonderful news," said a very excited King Bellorus as the old king bit his nails and coughed uncontrollably.

King Braithwaite rubbed his tummy and scratched his rusty beard waiting to hear what his underling had discovered. It was a heavily loaded morning with the discovery of Valkin Kendor. King Braithwaite had decided to continue his plan. They had just finished eating breakfast. He was taking full advantage of King Gilleus's hospitality. He even had the audacity of sitting in King Gilleus's royal chair. King Gilleus didn't mind. They were good friends with each other. They didn't care about formalities. Gilleus knew he couldn't afford to be an enemy of Sarcodia, especially with King Braithwaite sitting on its throne. Even with his large army, he still would not be able to match the strength of Sarcodia even if he wanted to defy him. More importantly, their friendship went back many years. It was only the three of them sitting around a small round table.

Prince Michael was still fast asleep in his royal chambers as was always the case with the young and restless royalty having no care in the bloody world.

"Well out with it Bellorus!" asked King Braithwaite with noticeable urgency.

Bellorus's thin, hunched 5.2 ft height and meager 150 lb weight enticed King Braithwaite into being so hasty. His settled ash-grey eyes and pale white skin clung onto the remnants of a once bustling life but now, after having the orange juice of life squeezed out of himself and his kingdom, he found himself perpetually drained and always trying to please.

"We followed Friedrich until he had reached Razortor precisely at midnight. Then, something strange happened to him and his horse. They both began to glow and then they began to run faster than our normal horses could match and suddenly disappeared out of sight in a flash. We tried to follow them but they were too far ahead already. I've never seen a horse move that fast before, King Braithwaite," replied Bellorus with some concern in his voice at the anomaly, he witnessed the night before.

King Braithwaite stroked and twirled his rusty beard as he leaned back into his chair forming a relaxed pose then he put his two hands together and intertwined his fingers before unlocking his fingers and started to finger tap upon his armrests. He was preparing to answer with a big smile on his face.

"And you never will, good Bellorus for you have been deceived by magic, good friend. That was no horse! That was a wolf! In fact, that was the lord of all wolves, *Rufor Rafelieus* himself," smiled King Braithwaite.

King Gilleus inhaled as he crept backward in his seat turning to see King Bellorus's reaction.

"Rufor Rafelieus, the Lord of all Wolves. But that would mean..." Bellorus paused at that moment finally figured it out and was on the same page as everyone.

King Braithwaite nodded wiping his mouth with a clean white napkin and stood up dragging the royal oak chair behind his back to allow him the space to approach his subject.

"Yes our champion, Friedrich is also a good friend of Vallentors and we didn't even know it. Haha! Well, we did in a way through my daughter. I can scarcely believe that I actually shook hands with one of my greatest enemies; but of course, I knew that from the beginning." King Braithwaite smiled and returned to his seat grabbing a grape from a bowl of fruit laid before them consisting of many other types of exotic fruits from pomegranates to strawberries. "Any ideas, on which direction he could have gone after you lost him?"

"Hard to say, my lord! He vanished from our view within seconds. Those wolves are incredibly quick! Our horses were no match for them!" Bellorus was wallowing in astonishment and disappointment.

"They are indeed. Horses, horses, fucking horses," replied King Braithwaite rolling his eyes upwards with some agitation in his voice. "Fucking boring creatures they are! Only good for meat and menial tasks! They are not bred for war. Perhaps in time, that problem will be rectified," uttered King Braithwaite with sinister intentions behind his words as King Bellorus smiled to himself.

King Gilleus brought the discussion back to the major matter at hand.

"Do you know his name good king, this boy called Friedrich?" asked King Bellorus with great interest.

Braithwaite creased his lips, looked up at the ceiling, and replied,

"Yes, I do and you won't believe who he is, Bellorus. His name is Valkin, Valkin Kendor."

King Bellorus's eyes widened with horror as he digested what King Braithwaite had just said finding the courage to reply. "He is the son of Helleus Kendor?"

"Yes!" Braithwaite was trying to make sense of everything. He stood up and walked to a window allowing the fresh morning breeze to gently brush his face and refresh his weary mind. "Gentlemen, we cannot speculate any further. Whether Vallentor has allied with the DallaVegans or not, I think that the DallaVegans should be crushed anyway. Their city borders Hallucagenia on the northeastern side. If we take them out, Aglypha will have free passage through the ruins straight into Hallucagenia. We will then launch our attack from the southeast." King Braithwaite then turned to face Bellorus with expectation. "Bellorus, what is the latest on the horses? Please, fill King Gilleus in here."

King Gilleus was still in a bit of shock as he came back from his bewilderment to the real world to listen again to the conversation. Gilleus stroked his falcon beard and felt clueless as he creased his aged white eyebrows waiting for Bellorus to elaborate on the latest developments on his front.

"Yes, my Lord. With pleasure! You have heard of the legendary line of magicians, we possess?"

"Yes, actually I have. Their experiments have caused much controversy in the past. Oh yes, I'm familiar with the giants of the Black Forest! They were also responsible for most of the giant creatures we see here today in our lands. What are they up to now?" asked King Gilleus with intrigue in his hazy blue curious eyes.

"Something unbelievable! I have ordered a recall of every horse loaned or bought within our three kingdoms. Of course, the owners will be adequately compensated for their sacrifice with strong donkeys."

"Seems like an ass of a deal but continue! What's the plan for those horses, Bellorus?" King Gilleus looked intrigued and wanted to know more.

"The magicians are going to change them," replied a very calm King Braithwaite.

"Change them? Into what?" Gilleus didn't like the sound of it but Braithwaite was savoring every moment of it as Bellorus continued.

"It was found that armor and speed are great stumbling blocks within our army as King Braithwaite alluded to earlier, severely slowing us down and giving the enemy the advantage. My apparent failure to apprehend the fugitive Valkin bares testimony to our weakness. This proved to be the final key point leading up to the decision which I might add was not taken lightly by King Braithwaite and myself! So, to explain what the magicians did was fuse the blood of the wolves with that of the horses. This allowed a rapid increase in their speed and aggression making them more faster and vicious. An obvious side effect is a change in their physical appearance, but I'm told that would not be a problem. I'm told that they have the paws of wolves & thus the speed of the wolves but the body and head of a horse. Their coats are shaggy and shiny which will greatly protect them on the battlefield. They are unlike anything you could ever possibly imagine. I have not seen the preliminary results of the experiments, but I'm told that they are truly amazing creatures. I must say, to be surrounded by such talented magicians is truly an honor. Secondly, fitting armor to horses is cumbersome and easily shed in battle, which is not ideal. The magicians have thus created an armor that is permanently part of the creature's body. It spontaneously forms during stressful situations and in battle and uses the ground as an energy source. The armor itself originated from the ground. The base substance was kindly provided by the ground elemental, Groudenor. It will form a protective shield and solidify around the creature's body giving it a rock-hard appearance. The best part is that it is as strong as ashblock and replenishes itself when it flakes off during battle blows to it. So even if your men die, the bloody fucking creature will take over and fight for you. That's if the magicians can perfect their training and control."

"It sounds macabre and bizarre but I guess anything to give us the added advantage to win this looming war," replied a worried Gilleus. Braithwaite came up behind him and tapped him on his shoulders.

"Don't worry too much. I know how much you love horses. It would be better for them this way. They have a better chance of surviving and we will have a better chance of living. I've spared a few to roam the northern planes if it makes you feel better, King Gilleus," smiled Braithwaite turning to Bellorus, "Thank you Bellorus. I have one more request."

"Yes, my Lord," replied the skulking figure of Bellorus.

"Inform Lord Revengor to prepare his legion. We attack at sunset tomorrow!"

"Yes, my Lord," smiled Bellorus.

King Gilleus was shocked at King Braithwaite's declaration. He wanted to know more about when King Braithwaite secured an alliance with the dragons of Razortor but knew that asking him would be disrespectful and so he controlled his urge and kept quiet. He just wondered what King Braithwaite was up to.

Where in the world is Valkin at a time like this?

"Good to have you back Rufor and not a moment too soon. We were almost done for there brother!" replied Valkin with a great big smile on his face.

They were on their way through the Pine forests.

"Thanks, Valkin, it's bloody good to be back! The Pine forests restore my strength and vigor and not to mention the spell wearing off. This is why I hate magic. You could say that again, that was close," replied the big wolf relieved to have returned to his original form. The two were traveling non-stop through the night through the forest and they were growing tired.

"So where are we going, if I may ask?" asked a perplexed Valkin.

Rufor kept silent for effect and then replied. "DallaVega."

"What's a DallaVega? Sounds like a vegan who you don't want to mess around with," replied Valkin chuckling to himself.

"Haha! Very funny! It's the name of a hidden city in the middle of the Pine Forests."

"Strange! I have never heard of it before."

"Not many have. The DallaVegan history and city were buried in the deep recesses of the minds who those who barely remember her. No accounts of it will be found in books or maps. As I said, very few know about this place and the few that do know are both friends and foes. Anyway, what news from your side? Did you find out who shot the princess?" asked Rufor as he ran as fast as he could through the forest. His massive 12 ft tall, 2-ton frame powered through the denser parts of the forest with ease and grace.

"Well, I found out that one Kendrick from Sarcodia could have been responsible for the attempt on Lady Melody's life back at the gauntlet."

"What makes you say that, Valkin?"

"Well, after the tournament ended, I collected the money and promised to give it to him as an act of charity. We had talked about it before the tournament and he told me a story about what he would do with the money. He said he'd give it to his mom and I thought that was an admirable thing to do, so when I won, I tried to find him after the tournament but he was nowhere to be found. Why would anyone turn their backs on a guaranteed twenty thousand zafrith? That just doesn't make sense to me. That's why I think he's a likely suspect."

"Maybe, maybe. I overheard Braithwaite saying something very disturbing. He said that he 'sees that Raven hasn't lost his touch.' I don't know what he meant by that. Whether or not he figured out our plan or whether Vallentor instructed Raven to take the shot, I'm honestly not sure. I really don't know how much to read into that statement, Valkin." Valkin was taken aback by what Rufor said about it being Vallentor's plan to assassinate Lady Melody.

"The plot thickens Rufor! I guess both possible suspects are hard to blame since there's no real evidence that they shot the arrow, none that I could see anyway. It could have been anyone and Braithwaite could have been referring to an incident that happened a week ago for all we know with regards to Raven. Interesting to say the least though, hey Rufor?"

"True. What does this Kendrick fellow look like anyway?"

"Tallish guy. Wore the grey and black colors of Sarcodia. That's all I know."

"Well, that's funny you mention it. Is, that him, up ahead, Valkin?"

Valkin squinted his eyes and looked carefully ahead. He could barely make out the colors of the rider but he could see the grayish tinge and cloaked hood in the early morning sunlight.

It was Kendrick!

Valkin confirmed it.

"Yah! That's him alright. Stay a little back so the bastard doesn't realize we're following him."

Rufor shook his head and slowed down a bit, maintaining the same pace as the speedy midnight black horse that Kendrick was riding. He must have left shortly after breakfast from some Inn he stayed at the night before.

"What a strange coincidence. He's also going to this place DallaVega," smiled Valkin.

"I reckon things are about to get very interesting in DallaVega. That quiet city is not going to be quiet for very much longer, Valkin."

The forest trees were whizzing past them in flurries of shamrock green and butterscotch yellow as the sun was brightening and dimming through the thin slits of space between the dancing leaves.

"Hey Rufor, you didn't mention why we were on our way to DallaVega man?"

"No I didn't, did I. Well, Donavan DallaVega, the ruler of the kingdom was not of your concern up until now. Vallentor didn't see fit to tell you about his brother just yet."

Valkin almost fell off Rufor when he mentioned 'brother'. He was shocked! He couldn't believe that Vallentor actually had a brother and kept it a secret from him.

"HIS WHAT!" replied an astounded Valkin.

"Yes, his younger brother. Donavan is Vallentor's younger twin brother but they were separated soon after birth and have grown up in completely different kingdoms. As a result, they don't exactly get along with each other."

"Very, very interesting! But why would he want to assassinate Princess Melody? What's in it for the DallaVegans except for war? I don't understand it."

"Well, we don't really know that it was him for sure, Valkin. Kendrick could be anyone but the fact that he's running in the direction of DallaVega; he's likely a DallaVegan assassin and if he is the one who shot the arrow then you're right about this city not being quiet anymore."

"He must have done it, Rufor! But how, who shoots an arrow, and gets away to a city that technically doesn't exist? It's the perfect crime and he's the perfect villain!"

"Mmm...it can't be that simple. Why would a city that virtually doesn't exist want to get roped into a war that isn't theirs to fight? I'm willing to guess that there's a lot of money involved here and if there's one thing I know about these DallaVegans, is that they love money!" Rufor's rhetorical question and declaration got Valkin thinking.

"Let's figure it out when we get there. Perhaps you could tell me why Vallentor and Donavan were separated at birth?"

"From what I know, Donavan & Vallentor were born on the first night of the fourth sun cycle. This meant that they were inextricably linked to the power of the Burning Desire."

"The Burning Desire to do what exactly?" asked a completely puzzled Valkin.

"No, No," chuckled Rufor. "Let me explain. The Burning Desire is a rare power given to twins allowing them to control a particular element. The burning desire has profound cycles where the elements of water, wind, earth, and fire are expressed. It just so happens that the powers bestowed in that cycle were that of fire."

"It seems that finding out who shot Melody isn't the only thing we're going to be doing in DallaVega, are we?"

"Damn straight lad! Now you talking! If the two were reunited, they will become an incredible force to be reckoned with! Even, the great fire elemental, Falkarnor who still fights for Braithwaite, could easily be destroyed. King Braithwaite knows this. But what he fears the most is the DallaVegans allying with us and that's why he wishes to destroy DallaVega now and kill Donavan before moving onto us. It's one less nuisance to deal with in his campaign to take over the lands."

"Still, that doesn't explain the assassination attempt. Anyway, why didn't Vallentor and Donavan ever make any attempts to get along? They live so close to each other and they are brothers after all. If they could be a force to be reckoned with, I would think at least getting along is a must."

"They chose not to. Donavan was plunged into a world of extreme violence, power, and money whilst Vallentor was exposed to injustices and politics through the old council of Lataria. Vallentor grew up in Lataria and Donavan in DallaVega. They came to know of each other's existence not ten years ago and immediately understood the need for them to keep their distance from each other. Ironically, DallaVega and Hallucagenia are neighbors but their kings are not so friendly with each other. Because they have chosen not to learn how to use the power within them, the power they possess cannot be harnessed nor controlled. They know this. They could potentially kill everyone around them including themselves if they ever released it without achieving some level of control."

"Is the hour too late for an alliance between Hallucagenia and DallaVega, Rufor?"

"If you ask me, to answer your earlier question Valkin, about the assassination attempt, I think that alliance has already been made. Rather late than never hey," replied a somewhat concerned Rufor.

"The least we can do now is warn them about Revengor's imminent attack!"

"WHAT! That's a name I've heard before in the tales of Razorock! Revengor, the dragon-king! The demon-hunter who himself, is a demon! I've never seen Razortor Rufor and I don't ever want to see that place. In the tales, they say that it is hot and fiery, filled with rage and anger. Revengor's primitive dragons patrol the skies scorching anything that comes their way. Even the snakes of Aglypha are afraid to visit that place."

"Ah! So, you've heard some stories about the great Revengor and Razortor, have you? Good, good! Well, you'll get to meet him in person soon enough. Then, you can tell new stories to your kids. A lesson needs to be learned there, but first things first, Valkin; we need to find out who Melody's attacker was! Didn't you want to know who did it? You seemed very eager two minutes ago to find him," replied Rufor with a big smile.

Valkin's attention was now divided between the impending doom of Revengor and Melody's attacker as his mind filled with both fear and anxiety overflowing into the dirty brown sweat that he released into the fur of Rufor.

"Yes, yes Melody's attacker," replied Valkin half-heartedly.

Meanwhile, in DallaVega...

"So, Ordanian, did you get her?" asked a man with a very familiar-sounding voice and face. His dark brown hair and crystal fire eyes pierced through the vast extent of the DallaVegan lands. His anticipation was hidden behind his face of immense power and pride. He wore an open, pristine white tunic with a dark satin black and poison purple suede coat.

"Well, not exactly sir. Someone else shot her before I did."

The man turned around to face Ordanian still dressed in his Sarcodian cloak with a look of surprise on his face.

"Er hum! Excuse me!" asked the mystery man who was visibly not very pleased with the news as his surprise turned into obvious frustration. He wanted an explanation from Ordanian gritting his teeth overlooking the kingdom of crystals holding the stone balcony with crushing fists.

"It's true. Someone actually split my arrow and shot the girl with the same poison that arrows are laden with. There must be a spy within our ranks," replied Ordanian with a look of deep disappointment upon his face as he bowed his head feeling bad for his king whose 6.2 ft frame looked down upon his smaller 5.3 ft, 154 lb frame.

The middle-aged man walked up to his subject and smiled at him.

"No, there isn't. It is entirely my fault my good Ordanian. The link between my brother and myself had become stronger of late. Damnit! I don't fucking believe it!" The man clenched his fists and turned away from Ordanian to face his kingdom which was beautifully decorated with Perusium crystals and colorful citizens pacing the walkways to their destinations. He turned to face Ordanian once again. "Ordanian, inform the elites and prepare yourself! We are going to have some uninvited guests visiting us today. Please will you make them feel welcome!" smiled the man. He then walked away from the balcony and the visage of his kingdom.

he Fields of Iriseae

The Pine forests suddenly ground to an abrupt halt as the two warriors reached the end of their journey. They waited outside the boundary separating them from their sparkling destination. The endless fields of Iriseae that lay before them were as tall as young pine and oak saplings, some 32 ft in height and filled with the lush colors and radiant blooms of the morning beauty. A 'circle' some called it, others knew it as a beautiful circle of silent sleep and death! A purple haze with orange leaves and a riot of brilliant colors that could outdo any rainbow on any day dominated the boundary walls of the small but mighty DallaVega.

King Donavan was waiting together with his right-hand man Ordanian or better known as "Kendrick" as he named himself in the tournament.

Donavan had his arms folded and was standing on the porch of his guest house just inside the boundary of deadly Iriseae smiling at the advancing 'guests'. His fire-red eyes were closed as he was lost, deep in thought and contemplation. The wind blew his long, dark black hair streaked with a purplish tinge to it. It blew across his face and rustled his dark eagle grey and black goatee. His facial features were remarkably the same as his older brothers but a bit more rough and hardened. His black and purple overcoat was lined with silver trimming and the Perusium crystals itself shone with a velvety, extravagant brilliance in the day's sunlight.

Ordanian, who had no mask on now had very youthful features. However, he was very old, in his mid-thirties but many were fooled by his clean-shaven face and short blonde wedge-like haircut. He was wearing a black tunic as well as ocean-blue leather pants. His green eyes were wide open and stared into the fields watching and waiting. His quiver of blue arrows and his excellently crafted longbow made from the reinforced wood of the Pine forests was slung across his small but powerfully lean shoulders.

King Donavan's build was slightly bigger at 209 lb and much more muscular than his brothers. Donavan was unarmed and remained in his deep trance-like state with his eyes closed, also waiting.

"Okay, Rufor, got any ideas?" asked Valkin with his hands on hips as he examined the height of the lush and beautiful plants of the Iriseae fields.

"I'm guessing you've never crossed a field of Iriseae before. It's only twenty meters from the outside circle to the inner one. Just hold on tight Valkin and pray that we survive this," replied Rufor as he slowly backtracked.

Valkin tightened his grip on the syrupy brown reins and swallowed hard.

"How do you know that, Rufor?" asked a very concerned Valkin. He wondered what all the fuss was about! They were just plants, beautiful plants as well.

"I've been here before and the last time I was here, I nearly died," replied Rufor.

"WHAT!" replied a surprised Valkin as he almost rolled off the back of an advancing Rufor who suddenly took off with great speed. Rufor sped towards the cliff's edge and leaped into the air. Soon, they were airborne and increasing in altitude fast. Valkin expected to see the entirety of the kingdom but what he got was a shock instead.

"Er' erm Rufor, what's happening to the fields? Why are they moving? Plants aren't supposed to move right? OH SHIT!!!"

Rufor and Valkin were floating in the air amidst blue skies and treacherous grounds below.

Rufor smiled as he prepared his body for the onslaught that was about to hit them.

"Oh, I forgot to mention. The fields of Iriseae have a unique ability…" Valkin cut in before Rufor could finish his sentence.

"Er' Rufor no disrespect but those fields are about to share that unique ability with us. If you'll allow me to be the gardener for the day?"

"With pleasure," replied Rufor as he smiled at the approaching Iriseae.

Plants are indeed alive but the Iriseae are truly living beings attacking anything that they perceive to be a threat to them or the people they protect. They first shot to the sky like spears to a target, piercing through flesh and bone impaling their victims with their harpoon flowers.

"Quickly Valkin! Get under me and use your sword. It's quicker!" Valkin held the reins and jumped off the right side of Rufor holding on to them tightly with his sword in his other hand. His eyes were fixed on the fast-approaching Iriseae plants. Just a trickle of sweat rolled down his face but quickly evaporated in the wind.

"Relax, Valkin, just cleave cleanly without cutting me ok," replied Rufor as he spread his paws out to catch more air in an attempt to slow down their descent.

The plants swished and hurtled through the air towards them screeching and hissing as snakes would do when cornered. Their flowers suddenly opened up and exposed an extremely sharp poisonous barb within. The Fields of Iriseae usually attack in waves. Each wave consisted of twelve plants extending wildly from the earth.

Valkin tightened his grip on the reins and held his sword tightly in final preparation for his assault. He couldn't see ahead of him. The plants were blocking his view and so he left Rufor to navigate and cover him.

Donavan's eyes were still closed and Ordanian looked on watching the entire aerial battle. Everything seemed to slow down as the plants approached the warriors. They got bigger and more menacing as they drew closer to Rufor and Valkin.

SLICE!

Valkin took out six in one go. The other six backed off and Valkin quickly got a glimpse of the kingdom in that brief moment. It was beautiful! Perhaps, one of the most beautiful kingdoms he had ever seen. It looked like ice crystals from the icy regions in the north that he used to read about when he was a child. The jagged ice-like crystals were Perusium buildups that grew over time. The city was built inside and around the Perusium deposits.

Valkin's beautiful view was suddenly cut off by the six remaining Iriseae which were targeting Rufor now. The two warriors were starting to descend now and fast too.

Rufor saw two coming at him, straight for his left eye. He shifted his head and bit into the side of the plants that came for him.

Valkin sliced through three on Rufor's right.

Rufor didn't even know about the three plants on his right. Valkin quickly sheathed his sword. The last one was heading straight for Rufor's forehead. Valkin saw it and swung backward quickly, still holding onto the reins, and jumped in front of Rufor catching the plant in his bare hands and ripping it from its stems just before it struck Rufor. Valkin swung around and landed back on the saddle with the squirming plant in his hand just as they landed in front of the crystal guest house, about 32 ft away from where Donavan and Ordanian were standing with a loud thud that shook the earth beneath them.

Ordanian had his bow unslung and fitted with a blue arrow pointing straight at Valkin.

Rufor didn't like the situation one bit.

Valkin was still holding the severed squirming plant, which he threw to the floor in front of him. He then looked at the structure before him and admired it. It was out of this world. The two doors were made from gold and the rest of the structure was made of Perusium.

Suddenly, Rufor shouted to Valkin.

"VALKIN, LOOK OUT!"

Valkin heard the release of Ordanian's hands and turned to find an arrow hurtling toward him at an incredible speed. Valkin had just enough time to draw his sword and use it to block the arrow, which was aimed at his heart. Valkin then didn't even register Ordanian's next movement from the porch to the edge of the fields where he released another arrow. Valkin just wasn't fast enough but strangely enough, he instinctively bent his body backward allowing the arrow to wiz past him. Valkin's body was moving by itself.

Donavan's fire-red eyes were still closed and his arms were still folded.

Ordanian was impressed at Valkin's agility. Ordanian, under usual circumstances, never failed to hit his target the first time. It was difficult for him to digest two failures back-to-back.

Rufor's gaze was only upon Donavan. He wasn't too interested in the battle between Ordanian and Valkin.

Suddenly, at least five Ordanians were surrounding Valkin and Rufor. Valkin shifted from left to right dodging arrows. He jumped up and dived to the ground and at times was rolling all over the place.

Donavan then began to laugh. He suddenly opened his eyes and his piercing gaze released wind-like energy that knocked Valkin back completely off his feet. The energy only rustled Rufor's fur. Apart from that, it did not perturb the lord of all wolves
. Once Valkin recovered and stood up, Donavan said to Ordanian in his deep and powerful voice, which matched his brother's perfectly.

"Stop playing around, Ordanny."

It was only at that point that Valkin realized the identical resemblance that Donavan shared with his brother, Vallentor. His features and his voice were one and the same. Valkin was shocked for a moment, too shocked to react to anything knowing that he was being toyed with whilst giving it all he had. He couldn't even register any of Ordanian's next movements now and he felt a very cold chill run up his spine as small trickles of sweat ran down his face and body whilst he still shivered. He felt the arrow tip strike his heart a thousand times but in reality, it didn't hit him once. Valkin's eyes turned to his right and he heard Ordanian whisper strikes. He then saw Ordanian appear on his right-hand side in the corner of his eye. The arrow was now aimed at the side of his head. Ordanian then appeared and said 'strike' again. Valkin could hear the arrow pierce through his flesh but again nothing was happening in reality. It was all in his mind. Suddenly, Ordanian's body disappeared and appeared on Valkin's left with the arrowhead pointing at the other side of Valkin's head. Ordanian said 'strike' again! Again, Valkin had to go through the agony of a similar strike to his head. Suddenly, Ordanian disappeared but Valkin didn't realize it until he saw

Ordanian walking back toward Donavan. Ordanian put his right leg on the porch, stopped, and turned around to face Valkin and Rufor. He had his bow in his left hand and there was no arrow in his right. All his arrows were still in his quiver. It was as if he never drew any from the beginning. There was no smile on Ordanian's face but there was a smug smirk on Donavan's.

That was Ordanian, "Ordanian of The Quick Return" they called him. He was so fast that he could retrieve any arrow that missed its target, put it back in his quiver, and fire it again. It was no illusion. He was just unnaturally fast! The scary part was that he was nothing compared to some other warriors out there.

Valkin was in a deep state of shock. His mouth was slightly opened as he stared blindly into the distance trying to comprehend what was going on. He wondered how could a man be that fast.

Ordanian then said to him as if answering his questions. "Yes, boy I could have killed a thousand times and you wouldn't have even known about it."

At that declaration, Valkin fell to his feet holding his sword tightly, and began to weep softly with the fear and horror of the predicament he found himself in. His sword hit and pierced the ground burying half of itself within in an exclamation of defeat.

Rufor then nudged Valkin with his snout in an effort to cheer him up.

"Come on boy, get up quickly! Turn around! Quickly now, saddle up. They're almost here... Ahh! Finally!"

Valkin opened his tear-filled eyes and smiled at Rufor momentarily.

Rufor crouched low allowing Valkin to climb upon his back.

Donavan's smirk vanished as he and Ordanian also vanished from the guest house in the blink of an eye.

Rufor suddenly jumped high up into the air. Valkin had to hold on for dear life.

The guest house suddenly exploded below them and was reduced to nothing but a pile of rubble.

As Rufor and Valkin descended, two figures appeared from nowhere. Their large dark silhouettes were hazy in the mini dust storm that the explosion created. Valkin coughed with his eyes closed as Rufor smiled at the clearing storm. Once again, the blue skies above appeared and so did Vallentor and the Death Brothers, Raven, and Marve Ominous following him. They had arrived with Pixie and Mike as reinforcements.

Donavan was standing before them with his arms folded once again, smiling.

The seven warriors suddenly realized that they were surrounded by DallaVega's elite strike force. A formidable force of a hundred men armed with bows slung and ready with deadly Iriseae poisoned tipped arrows. They were all dressed in sapphire blue and peace white with their heads covered in white veils. Their targets were confirmed.

Vallentor was leaning on his saddle as the Death brothers surveyed their surroundings.

Donavan had them right where he wanted them and he knew it but he didn't know that Vallentor came with some backup of his own as well.

Smoke rose from the edge of the outer circle. It was a highly controlled fire that was burning only a small section of the field not more than four meters wide making a distinct clearing through it. The fire drew closer and closer and the smoke veiled another mysterious warrior's silhouette. His eyes were on fire when they should have normally been neon green. His hair was also on fire when it also should have been a passionate green of power and fluidity. He burned a neat line, right through the fields making a pathway as a result of his foreboding 7 ft tall figure that waltzed through it. The winds then picked up behind him and blew away the smoke to reveal a somewhat disturbed but determined Tereartre Levon. The point of his arrowhead was on fire as he aimed it at the ground where he then stood waiting for anyone to make the slightest move.

Donavan put his arms to his side and walked forward towards Tereartre.

"So it was you who destroyed my beautiful guest house. You're going to pay for that, Dark Knight. Oh, I know you can't because you don't have enough money so you're going to have to pay with your life?"

Tereartre didn't even bother looking at Donavan and he didn't even bother to respond. Tereartre's gaze was fixed on the elite forces who were mumbling amongst themselves.

Their bows drooped slightly and their firm stance slackened a bit. They knew exactly who Tereartre Levon was and they knew of his terrible might! They knew him all too well, as the commander of the

Werethallic Wolf Forest Force, and better known as one of the greatest Dark Knights alive today. It was not in any elite force's psyche to back down without being given an order from their leader and the elite forces of DallaVega, although evidently rattled, were no exception. However shit scared they were, they held their ground, a mark of a truly elite force.

Tereartre Levon kept his eyes alit with fury and disgust at Donavan.

Valkin, who still was on Rufor, kept quiet and admired the Werethall leader, whom he had never seen in this Dark Knight form up until now. Nonetheless, he somehow knew that it was massively powerful. He could feel it! He could sense it!

"Put down your bloody weapons, warriors. They come in peace," shouted Donavan in a sarcastic manner as he spun around to face Vallentor.

Vallentor disembarked from Mike and walked towards Donavan, his twin brother, who also walked towards him.

Tereartre calmed down and so did his mystical flames, which simmered off into thin air revealing his long green hair once again. He put his arrow back with the rest in his quiver and slung his bow around his shoulder.

Ordanian gritted his teeth and clenched his fist and then released it shifting his gaze towards Donavan. It irritated Ordanian to know that as strong as he was, he was far more inferior to the strength of Tereartre Levon than he could imagine but he kept his nerve and his cool.

Raven & Marve were standing next to each other behind Vallentor with snug smiles on their faces.

Vallentor broke the silence first. "Aren't you glad to see me, brother? We came all the way from Hallucagenia to help you and this is the reception we get."

Donavan smirked at his brother's words. "Let me remind you Vallentor, that it was your man who blew up my building and foiled my plans and you're talking about warm receptions. You're an idiot, you know that! You could have killed us all, the Perusium in this area was unstable," replied an irritated Donavan with his hands in his pockets.

"Perusium is the least of my concerns. Your wild weeds tried to kill two of my good men. I'd say we're even. Besides, you're so filthy rich, you can build another hundred of these precious little guest houses.

However, I am the one who foiled your plans. That you can blame me for," replied Vallentor admitting to the crime he was being accused of. The two looked almost exactly the same.

It was very weird for Valkin to see them having it out like this. He expected a much better relationship but then again, he wasn't surprised that it had deteriorated to such an extent against the backdrop of Rufor's back story surrounding these two.

"The wolves don't count, do they, Vallentor?" replied Donavan with a smirk on his face.

The hundred strong men suddenly surrounded the six warriors with their bows slung and aimed square for their heads.

Rufor, Raven & Marve then started to laugh.

Marve had to say something. "Hey Vallentor, your brother has a wicked sense of humor." Marve then broke out into a burst of furious laughter and the others followed suit except for Tereartre who just smiled.

Vallentor walked around Donavan who stood in the same position and put his hands on his hips. "My dear brother, to judge someone by their appearance is very foolish and naïve. One should judge someone based on their character and the substance of their heart. The shallowness and egocentric behavior of today's leaders amazes me. Their lack of profoundness and depth impedes their personal growth and prevents them from opening their eyes to the wisdom that surrounds them. I will gladly die for Rufor Rafelieus for he is my brother, not some mindless animal of which there are plenty in our humanly 'higher' places. What is sad in this world is that your own kin treat you like fucking rubbish! The wolves are more loyal like their ancestors and are unwavering in their disposition. Maybe you should learn this lesson from them brother!" Vallentor glinted with anger in his smoke-grey eyes.

"Your words fall upon deaf ears, brother! If it's the power of the 'Burning Desire' you seek, then you have come to the wrong place for I am not interested. You could die for all I care," replied Donavan turning his back on his own brother and walking away back towards the inner safety of his beloved kingdom, DallaVega.

"Is that the way you talk to your elder brother? Besides, that's not the only thing that I'm interested in. I want to know why you wished to kill the Princess. Who put you up to it and what's in it for you brother?" Vallentor had a beady-eyed look.

Donavan gritted his teeth causing his cheeks to swell a little but he kept quiet and only after some time he spoke out.

"Look, brother, sooner or later, you will realize that there are bigger, more powerful Barargs in the fucking forest and then only, you will start to see my point of view. Revengor will be here anytime now? We're outnumbered and we are going to die because of our FUCKING EGOS! No amount of perusium will save us, nor our people. As for your sweet little princess, you should look around you more closely for the real perpetrator!"

Vallentor was perturbed by his brother's assertion about Princess Melody's shooter. He resolved to leave the discussion about the identity of the shooter unresolved and did not pursue it further.

"You cannot help us brother!"

"That's not entirely true. What about the bombs you've made? Their blast range is greater now?" asked Vallentor.

"What good are bombs if you can't use them, brother?" The look of despair upon Donavan's face was evident.

"What do you mean?" asked Vallentor with a confused look on his face.

"Our spies have told us that King Braithwaite has issued an order to summon the Aglyphan army as well. That's not all. Falkarnor will be joining them too after the dragons have had their way with our city. This is the penultimate episode for DallaVega, Vallentor. Our time has come." Donavan closed his eyes and swallowed hard knowing that his beautiful kingdom was going to be destroyed in a matter of a few hours.

Vallentor's head tilted back slightly as he took in the magnitude of the new problem. He knew that he could not take on the combined forces of Razortor and Aglypha, not to mention Falkarnor, the second most powerful elemental next to Rehowlor. Everyone was a bit jittery after Donavan's statement, even Valkin who realized that he was about to become a soldier in a war that he still didn't know why he was fighting for.

"Look, we have two choices..." smiled Donavan. "The first is, we choose to litter the fields of Iriseae with the blood of the dead bodies of all kinds or we do the one thing that I simply detest but I know will save us for now." Donavan sighed shaking his head. "We must embrace the power of the Burning Desire. They're coming to kill us all, Vallentor! They know I'm here & they know I'll help you but what they don't know is in what way. At least, we have that element of surprise in our favor. Perhaps for peace, we should use it to kick the shit out of the bastards!" Donavan gave out a huge sigh and pondered about the idea for a minute or two whilst the others waited for a reply. The silence seemed long and filled with doubt and uneasiness.

Then, suddenly Vallentor spoke at last breaking the silence.

"Donavan, the last time we used that power was when we were born. We destroyed an entire city with it. Everyone died that day when we were born, even our mother and father. We were just newborns and we couldn't control the power. What makes you think we can do it now? Upon reflection, it's just too risky."

"Hey, this was your idea, brother. True, but have you ever wondered under what circumstances that power was unleashed."

Vallentor began to wonder and recollect his thoughts and then realized what Donavan was talking about. Everyone was puzzled. "That power was unleashed in all its fury because of the close bond we shared at the time."

"How do you know so much, Donavan?" asked Vallentor.

"Don't play coy brother. You know why," replied Donavan. "I was told by a wise man from the Dynasty," replied Donavan deep in thought.

"The Dynasty! You have been to the Dynasty, when?" exclaimed Vallentor. A collective chill went down everyone's spine except Tereartre and Valkin. Tereartre knew about the Dynasty. Valkin didn't know anything about it and didn't react.

"Yes, but perhaps that is a story for another time, assuming we survive this ordeal. Anyway, it is time for us to fuse my brother. I can hear the fluttering wings of the dragon king growing louder and louder with each passing moment." Donavan looked up into the sky and focused his attention.

The dragon king was indeed coming and he wasn't coming alone. Five of his strongest dragons were escorting the king through the sky. One dragon alone was enough to destroy a city. Revengor's fiery eyes were set on its distant target that he was fast approaching.

The wolves of the Pine forests were quick but they were no match for an aerial fight with dragons.

Revengor glared his teeth and pressed his advance towards DallaVega.

Donavan then opened his eyes as if resolved to the approaching doom and put his head down and looked at Ordanian.

Ordanian slowly nodded his head. He knew that this time would come.

Donavan walked up to Vallentor. He then turned around to face Ordanian one last time. "Ordanian, inform my people, will you, that you will take over rule of DallaVega in my stead. This is the last order I give you as myself." Donavan's voice was strong and determined.

Ordanian bowed, turned around, and walked to the ruins of the guest house. He lifted his right hand and the elite force that surrounded the warriors backed off to a mile radius within a few minutes.

Valkin was excited and walked up to Vallentor. Rufor tried to tell him to stop but he couldn't restrain him. Vallentor turned around to face Valkin.

Donavan looked at the approaching boy with a peaceful smile on his face. Valkin then stuck out his hands sensing something great was about to happen to them.

Vallentor received his handshake and greeted it with another. Valkin replied, "It's been an honor, sir. I hope we make it through this."

"I hope so too, Valkin?" replied Vallentor as he turned to face Donavan. "So, Donavan, are you ready?"

"There is no other way Vallentor. The dynasty said that the only way it will work is if our minds, bodies, and souls are in complete sync."

"Ok, how do we do that?" asked Vallentor.

"We must think about something, something extremely common to us. Our birth perhaps is the only thing common to us and then we just have to shake hands. That's it! That should release enough energy to initiate the fusion, or so I've heard. Haha!" There was a mischievous undertone to Donavan's laugh, which Vallentor did not appreciate.

Everybody stood back as Vallentor and Donavan began to synchronize their minds. It took a few minutes but then something started to happen. A pale sky blue and lime green hue of cloudy light began to encircle them and bind to their hands and foreheads. They began to scream in unison and then they slowly shook hands causing an explosion of crimson red energy to emanate from their beings that blasted most of the warriors back including Valkin.

Only the death brothers, Rufor, Tereartre, and Ordanian stood firm on their feet. The winds of energy only rustled their hair, a mark of their firm resolve and mighty strength.

Revengor was almost upon the gates of the kingdom when he saw the bright lights shine brightly before him. He smiled and said to his dragon companions in a low, sadistic voice.

"Looks like Falkarnor is going to have his hands full today."

Revengor's dragons squawked with laughter and then roared into the air announcing their unwelcome arrival to the people of DallaVega sending shivers of chilling fear down their scrambling spines.

Dark clouds overshadowed the streets below. Warning trumpets were blown warning people to stay indoors for their own safety. Panic and mayhem ripped through the streets as the tornado of panic set in through the fields of Iriseae.

Valkin was grounded and blinded by the bright red and white light that clouded everything. He squinted his eyes trying to make out what exactly was going on.

Then, a dark silhouette began to form from the very center of the light as it slowly diminished. Fiery red eyes that were closed for now readied themselves to be opened. Long red hair of shoulder length blew in the winds of energy created by this new being who wore singeing red armor that flashed on and off, with suede black pants and shiny black boots. His fists were clenched and his teeth were gritted.

The Death brothers were in awe and so were Valkin and Rufor. Tereartre had a humble look on his face. He heard legends of the power of the Burning Desire and its many manifestations but he did not realize that it was this powerful in its fully manifested form. He even contemplated fighting it, to see if it could match the strength of a Dark Knight.

The being then suddenly opened his eyes releasing a massive energy pulse that Valkin could barely prevent from toppling him over once again. Valkin covered his eyes protecting them from the dust and sand particles being swirled into the air and slowly lowered his hands to gaze upon this new being right in front of him. Valkin was startled and gritted his teeth but stood firm. He didn't register the movement of the being from where it was a mile away to where it was now, right in front of him. The being was tall, as tall as a barbarian at 7 ft! He was lean and mean! Valkin waited and so did everyone else in anticipation of what was going to happen next. They were so afraid that the being was unstable and going to explode. No one moved an inch.

Then, the being stretched out his hand in the form of a handshake gesture.

Valkin smiled and reciprocated.

Everyone breathed a sigh of relief.

The being also smiled baring his clean white teeth. The dark silhouette that shrouded his face revealed a red long coat and long black hair with a rusty brown tinge to it. Then, suddenly without warning, he spoke with a powerfully clear voice, which sounded like a mixture between Vallentor's and Donavan's. "So, what do you guys think of the new me?"

Everyone was too stunned to reply to them.

The two were now one! The being then looked up into the sky seeing something in the distance. He then looked back at Valkin. "You don't have to answer that question now."

Their enemies were approaching but only Tereartre and this new being knew that. The rest were oblivious to their approach. Only extremely strong warriors had the ability to sense the approach of other warriors, be they friends or foes. It is a skill that only the strong have mastered through many years of intense meditation and focus on their own energy. Every being emits an energy signal which can be detected and tagged to that individual. The strongest warriors have the ability to detect this energy trace from many miles away. It's like a wolf that can smell its prey from many miles away by tasting the air. However, one uses another sense to achieve this.

"What can we call you now, friend?" asked Valkin finally breaking the silence.

"Sorry, Valkin, no time for introductions!" The being clenched his fists and put them over his heart and closed his eyes.

The enemies were almost there, just a few miles away from DallaVega. The wings of fury and death were approaching and they were not alone. The king of the Serpentines, Arnaiboa was also with them and so was the "strongest" fire elemental, General Falkarnor.

The being then clenched his right fist and banged it against his chest once again and held it there. He slowly began to pull out an object from the depths of his chest. It was a glowing sword that seemed to originate from the lava of Volcanock herself. The lava flowed over the entire sword continuously but never overflowed to the ground. It was sharp and hot, as hot as a Dark Knight's sword.

Tereartre was curious but Valkin was intrigued. He wanted to see more from this being. He never knew of any such feat that any warrior could be capable of; materializing a sword from thin air! That was surely impossible.

The being just stood there facing his comrades with his eyes closed, sword in hand. His back faced the enemy. His front faced his friends.

Falkarnor, the fire elemental landed from the air. Falkarnor could heat the airwaves around him manipulating them to achieve flight. He was smiling as Revengor landed beside him. Arnaiboa had arrived too. Falkarnor's hair was permanently on fire. It burned brightly all the time and no one could get close to him, no one which was perhaps a blessing for him or a curse. He was the youngest and cockiest elemental, second only to Rehowlor in strength. His handsome and youthful features made him look far more innocent than he was but his arrogance defeated him to second place under the command of Rehowlor. He had the potential to be stronger than the wind elemental but he lacked experience in the faction of leadership He wore a tattered, faded red robe that covered his bare feet. It danced when the winds surrounding him began to pick up as he burned the surrounding remains of Donavan's guesthouse nearby him with pure heat alone. His striking blue eyes were a pair of flaming arrows that pierced through the warriors' lion hearts. Although they had never faced off against Falkarnor, they were unphased and respected his vicious reputation.

Revengor, on the other hand, was far older and more wrinkled around his forehead and upper cheeks. His face was half human and half dragon with gnarly horns jutting out of his leathery face and head. Sparse black hair lined his scaly head and flowed onto his thick neck. His lower enlarged canine fangs stuck out from his snout extending to his ringed nose, which snorted fire now and then. His outer hide bore a blood-red and leather-black speckled appearance, which faded when it met his broad, muscular chest. His golden-red wings stretched outwards to a resting wingspan of 16 ft and extended to the ground were neatly tucked away on his back. King Revengor made barbarians look like mere humans with his massive 10 ft frame. He was muscular and bulky but his half-human legs supported his heavy 440 lb weight as his hefty lizard-tail provided some balance to his sturdy, scaly footing. He was heavily armored on his back and legs but his six-packed abdominals were relatively bare. No one could ever get that close to him to make a dent into that relatively vulnerable part of his body. He was the King of Razortor, the land of dragons and fire. King Revengor stood proudly with his muscular arms to his sides and a large smile upon his crusty face. He was waiting for an invitation.

On the other hand, what Arnaiboa lacked in height, he made up in length. He was a 20 ft monster that was slithery, slimy pale green. The serpentines of Aglypha had lean and mean arms and legs protected by heavy armor and thick scales. Their appendages were rarely used for they preferred slithering around. However, their strength cannot be underestimated. The Serpentines looked like giant cobras poised to strike at any moment! An apt statement, as it was said, is that they are among the fastest-striking races in the world. They loved to kill without letting their victims know that they were already dead. Sometimes, they employed their favorite weapon, the Serpent's Leer. This was just to play with the victim for entertainment. The Gorillas of the Pine Forests, unfortunately, suffered greatly at the hands of the Serpent's Leer. It was a shocking reminder for the warriors and the elite force of DallaVega. The Leer hypnotizes its victim for a short time making them obey every command of the enchanter. It was said that Magnus, the great king of the gorillas withstood the Leer for many days after which he finally succumbed to the power of Arnaiboa himself.

The Burning Desire was still standing with his eyes closed and sword poised for action.

Falkarnor decided to break the ice with his firepower.

"HEY, WHAT ARE YOU WARRIORS WAITIIIINNNN..." Falkarnor did not have the opportunity to complete his sentence as he dropped his head and looked at the deep gash running across his torso, which started to spurt blood. Then, it started to ooze fire-red blood dropping him to the floor as he held his chest, choking and breathing heavily. Blood and fire flowed from the side of his mouth as his crimson red eyes looked to shock and disbelief.

Kings' Revengor and Arnaiboa looked at Falkarnor lying on the ground holding his torso, writhing in pain, and then looked at the Burning Desire in quite a surprised manner. They did not expect such power to flow from the Burning Desire, this quickly.

Falkarnor wondered what had just cut him. He looked around and saw King Revengor standing there with his arms folded with a very annoyed look upon his face progressing into a grimace. Falkarnor's eyes began to light up with a fiery glow as his anger levels began to increase. He got up and screamed as he blasted his way forward to take the Burning Desire head-on.

The Burning Desire was still standing in the same position as before not moving an inch.

Falkarnor's hands suddenly formed fire swords as tall as a human, which he swung together as he closed in on the Burning Desire. Falkarnor could then feel the warm prick of a seething sword sliding through his butter body. He then could feel his life slipping away from him at that very moment as the lava blade pierced right through his stomach cavity coming out through the other side.

The Burning Desire had his back turned on Falkarnor as Falkarnor fell slowly to his knees with the sword still stuck in him. The Burning Desire then slowly and carefully removed his sword from its victim causing minimal stress upon him. He flicked his sword to his right-hand side dispersing Falkarnor's blood upon the ground and held his sword firm.

Falkarnor held his stomach and grimaced with pain as he slowly rested his head on the ground and then fell to his side slipping into a deep unconsciousness.

"His wounds are not fatal. He is still alive!" replied the Burning Desire and then turning to Valkin he remarked, "Valkin, take him to the healer."

Valkin nodded and hastily ran up to Falkarnor and hoisted him up on his shoulders disregarding the blood dripping upon him. Valkin ran as quickly as he could to the healer who appeared from nowhere to assist.

The Death brothers were itching to jump into the fight but Tereartre's cool neon green eyes kept them at bay for the moment.

"Such ruthlessness Revengor, Arnaiboa. You ought to be ashamed of yourselves! Is this the way to gauge my strength or is it a testimony of your cowardice," asked the Burning Desire in a strong voice of conviction.

Revengor smiled and banged his head with his gnarly right-hand fist pulling out a monstrous 6.5 ft sword from his head. Its handle had beautiful molds of dragons that were laced with rubies and sapphire stones which pulsated a red and blue hue intermittently. The blade was coal black much like the menacing swords of the Dark Knights.

"Watch your tongue stranger! Don't think I don't know what just transpired before we arrived. Keep that in mind! I have seen many fusions in my lifetime, some of them I have affected myself and I'm not impressed," replied Revengor with anger and guile.

Raven and Marve were taken aback by Revengor's statements. They wondered if he was bluffing or if he was serious. Was the Burning Desire a shadow of the strength of himself and Arnaiboa, they thought? It certainly didn't feel that way or look that way, especially in light of how easy it was to dispatch Falkarnor.

"Lord Braithwaite is only perturbed by Helleus Kendor and no other! Bear that in mind, for that is why we all respected and feared him, and only him. We do not flinch in the presence of other beings who wish to emulate his strength or legacy. Pitiful weaklings like yourself are of no concern to us!"

"And what is the will of the great Lord Braithwaite now, may I ask? To kill and maim innocent people?" asked the Burning Desire.

Revengor smiled gritting his teeth and crunching on a few bones he had eaten for breakfast this morning.

"A strong message needs to be sent to the factions that wish to oppose the rule of our Lord and leader, King Braithwaite. As there will be sunshine after the rains, there will be casualties after the war. Some people need more persuasion to make up their minds. It would seem that the losses you sustained in the battle for the Pine Forests were not enough to wake you up. We are here as mere agents of persuasion who wish to make you see the light," replied the Razortorian king who then surged forward to meet the Dark Knightean sword of Tereartre's.

Tereartre lifted his head and looked at the giant frame of Revengor that towered above him. Both warriors' eyes then caught on fire as their swords sent sparks flying into the air reverberating a stalemate.

Arnaiboa who stood on the sidelines decided to get in on the action by testing his strength against the new warrior. He pulled out a very unusual-looking sword from his head. It was twisted and curved matching its wielder's dispensation. The handle ended with a snake's head sneering. The sword's dirty, muddy brown color resembled its wielder's shade of scaly skin.

The Burning Desire was open to an attack, as he watched Tereartre face off against Revengor.

Arnaiboa came towards him slithering on the ground at an incredible pace and as soon as he was in striking range he reared up his 20 ft long body and flared his hood hissing away at The Burning Desire. He slashed hard with his sword. The Burning Desire blocked the strike with his lava sword using only one hand. Arnaiboa towered over the Burning Desire and his 1000 lb weight began to place an intense amount of pressure upon the Burning Desire's spine. Their combined energies rustled the earth that surrounded them, blasting sand and dirt toward their sides sending goosebumps down the spines of the Death brothers who anxiously watched.

They smiled momentarily at each other with arms folded and observed the skies. Revengor flew into the air and hovered just above Tereartre's reach. He laughed at Tereartre. Tereartre's eyes could not be seen. The Dark Knightean fire oozed from it!

The Burning Desire's eyes could also not be seen for lava oozed from it but never fell beyond his cheeks. It just flowed and replenished itself constantly as he gazed at Arnaiboa who had a look of disgust on his slithery face.

Revengor swooped down on Tereartre who ducked and rolled to his left as Revengor flew around for another attack. The speed that Revengor was flying was incredibly fast. Tereartre looked up in the sky and screamed sending shockwaves that could be felt by the forces of a small force of serpentines and fire dragons that we just arriving on the scene now. The elite warriors did not come to the battle. Only the foot soldiers were ordered to come. They were feeling their first battle fear. The main reasons were because Tereartre was beginning to unleash his true power and the presence of the mysterious Burning Desire, a warrior they'd never seen before.

Tereartre from nowhere it seemed, was attracting armor to his body, the same type that was seen on the night of the sighting of Helleus Kendor, Valkin's father, and the fight at Gillmanor. He was attracting the sacred armor of a Dark Knight. It was a rare occurrence indeed and a spectacle. The only time a Dark Knight attracts the "armor of death" as it was called was when he's in trouble or wants to end the fight quickly. It's an extremely painful process to comprehend for an individual who's not a Dark Knight. The armor's origin is unknown. It is speculated that it originates from the God of Death himself but from where exactly it comes, is not known. As the individual parts of the armor, flew in dangerously from all directions, it could potentially kill anything that obstructed its flight path toward its master. The fusing of the armor with its master is the seemingly painful part. The inner side of the armor is coated with thin needles that pierce through the flesh but surprisingly, the Dark Knight sheds no blood nor does he feel any pain. If it was a normal man, he'd die instantly. The belief is that it pierces all pressure points numbing & releasing the devastating power within the knight's body. The best explanation is that the Dark Knights and their armor defy all explanations. The only thing that pierces a Dark Knight's armor is another Dark Knight's sword. The armor hits the bearer at an incredible speed. Each part fuses with its adjacent counterpart and seals itself immediately. All this happens in just a few seconds. The joins are sealed with fire.

Revengor was hovering above Tereartre, smiling at the upgrade his enemy had just made to his body. He slowly hovered to the ground and landed. Tereartre was ready to go! The fire was blowing out of his sight holes in his helmet. He hit his helmet and pulled out a black fire sword, which was burning for blood. Revengor merely laughed! Tereartre didn't like it! He rushed towards Revengor from the front leaping into the air. Revengor simply blocked the attack with his large broad sword flexing the muscles of his right arm as he did. He then hit Tereartre hard in the face with his left fist. Tereartre flew back toward the ground and tripped on a rock stumbling off his feet hitting the ground hard and being dragged backward by the force of the blow. Revengor then appeared next to Tereartre surprising him, catching his left hand, and then proceeded to swing him around in the air and smashed him into the ground creating a small crater in the ground. He then started to kick Tereartre's stomach further keeping him grounded. Each blow reverberated through every warrior's soul on the battle field. Tereartre's armor clanged and cringed and he could feel his heart racing to know that maybe, just maybe, his adversary could have grown to be just as strong as he was if not stronger. It had been a long time since Tereatre had fought an opponent of this high level of strength.

Some 320 ft meters away Arnaiboa gave the Burning Desire a head slash with his mysterious brown sword hissing at him bearing his deep dark throat of blackness. The Burning Desire blocked with his sword and fisted Arnaiboa in the stomach with his left fist. Arnaiboa bowed slightly choking on his blood after the severe blow as the Burning Desire jumped up and elbowed him to the ground. Arnaiboa hit the ground hard head first, eating dirt! The Burning Desire then lifted his sword readying himself for a beheading stroke but Arnaiboa rolled out of the way as the Burning Desire's sword hit the ground making a deep impression within it. Arnaiboa nipped up and kicked the Burning Desire in the face making him lose his grip on his sword and fly at an incredible speed toward the DallaVegan elite soldiers knocking out dozens of them in the process. Arnaiboa tried to grasp the Burning Desire's sword but the sword was so too hot to handle and it burnt him as soon as he touched it. He waved his hands in the air and blew into his scaly and now burnt brown hands to lessen the pain. The Burning Desire shook his head and gazed back at his adversary with disgust and guile as he leaned on the ground with his weary hands. His red hair blew across his face as his lava-filled eyes burned brightly. He got up and began to walk towards Arnaiboa who caught sight of him and readied himself for another round.

The Dark Knight armor usually repairs itself autonomously once damaged, but Revengor didn't give Tereartre a chance to heal himself. He kept on kicking and stomping away at the Fallen Dark Knight without any care or mercy. The entire ground was shaking showing the tremendous force with which Revengor was kicking Tereartre. With every kick, Tereartre sank half a foot deeper into the ground and the warriors all around were lifted a few centimeters off the ground as if there was an earthquake. The nerves of the elite DallaVegan soldiers were on the verge of breaking. They were literally in shock as to what they were witnessing before them! In some way, they were humbled by the great warriors of their time. Revengor was the kind of warrior who always wanted his adversary to experience extreme pain before dispatching them. He is purely sadistic by nature! Tereartre though, who was on the receiving end, just about had enough. He caught Revengor's next stomp just before it crashed against his chest and twisted Revengor's leg sending him rolling into the developing crater face first. Revengor recovered quickly but so did Tereartre. Tereartre got up and moved towards Revengor with great speed.

The Dallavegen elites could not follow their movements now. Only Ordanian, the Death brothers, and Rufor were able to register the fast-paced movements of the warriors.

Valkin, who returned from the healing house, could only manage to drool in awe but couldn't really see anything that was happening right before his eyes. He was just admiring the sight before him.

Tereartre readied himself for a straight side slash to Revengor's mid-section with his black Dark Knight sword which flamed around the edges menacingly. Revengor blocked the blow awkwardly and directed Tereartre's sword over his head. Revengor then caught Tereartre off his guard with a left hook to the ribs that rattled the Werethallic leader spurring him into a low leg sweep that dropped Revengor like a sack of potatoes to the ground. Tereartre jumped up and descended with a right knee primed for Revengor's head but missed as Revengor rolled out of the way. Tereartre's knee smashed into the ground cracking the earth wide open. Tereartre then followed that up with a slash to the rolling beast with his sword missing Revengor's tail by just a few inches. Revengor regained his senses and blew fire into the ground pushing himself up to help regain his footing and returned fierce blows with a side slash of his own which penetrated Tereartre's chest plate and sliced through the surface allowing flames and fire to flow out uncontrollably. Tereartre staggered back and held his chest tightly. Revengor straightened his stance and smiled breathing heavily. Tereartre smiled back.

On the other side of the grounds, Arnaiboa jumped up into the air and dived into the ground. The Burning Desire was taken aback by this strange ability and was soon also caught off his guard by an emerging snake king who uppercut him from the front driving his lower jaw hard into his top jaw jarring the Burning Desire's head backward. The Burning desire flew into the air and then hit the ground hard. The Burning Desire felt blood fill his mouth and then flow out through the sides. He wiped his mouth as Arnaiboa buried himself into the ground once more preparing for round two.

Suddenly, Arnaiboa emerged beside Revengor who then lifted his sword into the air. Time stood still for a moment or two and then the sword vanished from Revengor's hand. As soon as that happened, all the soldiers that came with them started to leave. The elite dragons flew off! Revengor and Arnaiboa bowed and then Arnaiboa jumped up into the air and then into the ground and swam away beneath it. Revengor spread his scaly and powerful wings and began to fly keeping his eyes fixed on Tereartre all the time never shifting his gaze. By this time, Tereartre's armor was completely repaired. Tereartre's armor began to turn into ashes and was blown away by a cool breeze that passed over the DallaVegan battlefield revealing his long green hair and cooling himself and the Burning Desire down.

Revengor was the last to leave. He grimaced at the two warriors and shrugged them off with a gesture as if to say that they were no match for them. He then flew away back towards the direction of Razortor.

Tereartre walked over to the Burning Desire and extended an arm out to formally greet him.

The others then joined them and briefed each other on their thoughts about the sudden end of the fight. Several whispers and low hushed talk reverberated all around DallaVega. Valkin was in shock as he stood just outside the DallaVegan elite soldier line. The Burning Desire called for him. Valkin couldn't hear the sounds around him. He was filtering them out. It almost seemed that he was in a world of his own for a moment when the faint mention of his name snapped him out of his trance-like state and he got up, dusted himself, and walked over to where many discussions were taking place. The crowds of warriors were on high alert for fear of Braithwaite's forces returning. The top warriors formed a half-circle comprised of Marve, Raven, Rufor, Valkin, Tereartre, and the Burning Desire. Rufor put in the first speculation.

"I think we should not be complacent, they might return and attempt to destroy this city or the forests. The path to Hallucagenia runs right through forests and the path through to the forests is through DallaVega.

They'll be back!" The Burning Desire's red eyes agreed with Rufor's hunches.

"I agree as well," replied Marve. "They didn't come all this way for nothing, did they? They're probably camping a couple of miles away from here. We should ready ourselves and send out a scouting party."

Raven didn't have an opinion yet. He was still assessing the situation.

Tereartre and the Burning Desire were just listening for now. Tereartre turned to the Burning Desire and decided to give his opinion.

"They won't be back. Not today, at least." Rufor shook his head in disagreement. "Rufor, you know that if they wanted to burn the forests down, they would have done so already."

Rufor hadn't thought about that.

"They were just testing us. Seeing how much we can handle. Waiting for us to go on the back foot."

Raven was unsettled by this declaration. He knew what it could mean for the warriors.

The Burning Desire then turned around and said to everyone present. "Perhaps. Then we must show them that when united, we can become a powerful force! Henceforth, the kingdoms of DallaVega and Hallucagenia are now one. Free travel to both kingdoms will now be permitted! Spread the word amongst the people and tell them that they fall under the protection of Hallucagenia from now on."

Tereartre kept quiet and assessed what the Burning Desire was saying and kept his thoughts still and private.

The Burning Desire then walked forward past everyone and went to investigate the damage to the DallaVegan kingdom. The guesthouse was totaled. The grass was no more. Part of the fields was burnt completely. That section of the kingdom was a complete mess. The Burning Desire looked at the place with sadness and said, "Where in the world am I going to start with the clean-up?"

Tereartre looked at the Burning Desire and inspected the damage and said to himself, "That must be Donavan's form speaking now." Tereartre smiled.

"Tereartre, what now?" asked Raven with a very serious look on his face looking for some direction from his fellow warrior.

"Take Valkin to Galapalau as soon as possible! He must meet the master! I'm going to have a little chat with the Burning Desire." Tereartre then turned to Rufor, "Will you and Marve please go back to Hallucagenia and ready half the army? Tell them to prepare especially for an aerial assault this evening as a precautionary measure. Then, move half of our legions to DallaVega's wall bordering Sarcodia. Also, please send out the scouts to follow those fucking dragons wherever they're going. Make sure they report back before nightfall or I'll kill them myself! They better be going the other way because if they are planning to come back, next time I won't hold back. I want a full report within the next two hours..." Rufor was about to speed off when Tereartre interrupted him once more, "Tell the rest of the army to fortify the Hallucagenian walls facing the Pine Forests."

Rufor and Marve sped off without question. They knew this precautionary measure had to be taken, even if no soldiers came this evening.

Tereartre then turned to Raven to give him his orders. "Take Pixie with you to the islands. She loves the beach! It will be good for her," requested Tereartre. "Take all that you require and leave within two hours." Tereartre then shook hands with Raven and Valkin and then turned around to meet the kingdom leader once again.

Valkin and Raven then moved off towards DallaVega to ready a pair of wolves to travel back home to Hallucagenia to make the final arrangements. The weather was now beautiful! Blue skies and a slow summer breeze blew across the faces of the many warriors to cool the situation down and blow away the smoldering fires that remained. Tereartre approached the kneeling Burning Desire who was inspecting the damage. The Burning Desire sensed the approach of Tereartre and got up turning around to meet him. "It's a mess Tereartre but at least there were no casualties?"

"That's always good! You've become much stronger, Vallentor, or should I say, Burning Desire. I can feel it!"

"Thanks," replied the Burning Desire who was inspecting himself. "I'm still getting used to it. To be honest, I am surprised it even worked considering our tragic track record. I believe there's more to this body than what I've shown. But, enough about me. How's Valkin doing? He looked a bit rattled back there."

"He's fine. He just had a wakeup call, that's all. He realized how weak he really was and how much stronger he still needs to get."

"Yes, yes!" replied the Burning Desire contemplating into the distance. His red hair flicked across his face in the wind. He turned to Tereartre and said, "Valkin doesn't even know it yet, does he?"

"No, he is unaware of it at the moment but the master will take care of that in time. He will determine its true nature, isolate it and deal with it. He truly is the master of our time. Under his wing and tutelage, Valkin will learn a lot," replied Tereartre with a stone look on his face. The Burning Desire looked in the direction from whence the dragons had come and folded his arms.

"He's driving us back with each incursion, Tereartre. I can't figure this man out. What does he want?"

"Well, revenge has always been high up on the list! I just hope that Valkin doesn't also add it to his list!" replied Tereartre in an ominous tone of voice.

The Burning Desire looked at Tereartre and then back towards the Pine forests.

*W*hen Valkin meets the master

"Valkin, how is he?" asked the Burning Desire entering the healing hut where Falkarnor was being healed by the barbarian healers. His body was in shock and broken and he was barely alive but only the Burning Desire's sympathy upon the battlefield saved him. His body was almost lifeless as he lay still on the bed with his eyes closed. The healers, a group of six elderly men with long white beards and wrinkled faces, surrounded the bed and emitted a halo of orange light from their hands, which was slowly healing the wounds inflicted upon Falkarnor by the Burning Desire. Valkin had a look of shock on his face as he witnessed what was happening before him. He wondered how the wounds within Falkarnor were sealing. What magic were these healers using upon him, he thought? How was this level of medicine possible? The world of Tillmandor seemed very small indeed and he was beginning to feel very grateful that he got the opportunity to get out, however, bizarre it seemed at the time.

"He is healing and getting better I hear from the healers," replied Valkin.

"Good, good. Listen Valkin. I'm sorry but we don't have much time to discuss anything in great detail at this stage. I have another mission for you, Valkin. It's more of a journey! I want you to go to an old friend of ours. He lives far beyond our Hallucen lands, on a small island within the Galapalaun island chain, called Gilipriel. This man will teach you the next set of skills that you will require on your journey in search of the answers to the burning questions you have within."

Valkin took a deep breath digesting the gravity of the next task that he was given by the Burning Desire.

"I already have so many questions that I'd like to ask you." The Burning Desire smiled.

"Go for it!"

"The first is what can I call you now?"

"The Burning Desire is our true name but you can call us Vallentorvan if you want. For now, Vallentor and Donavan are the same," replied the warrior of red hair and red eyes. He sported a rough beard and clean white shirt covered by a blood-red coat and raven black pants as well as iron black boots and stood much taller than Valkin smiling at him.

Raven just walked in and stood behind Valkin. "You called for me boss. What are your orders?" Vallentorvan walked over to Raven and held his shoulder almost whispering in his ear but kept his voice audible enough for Valkin to hear his plan.

"Raven, I need you to escort Valkin to Gilipriel. I think its time Valkin met the master. Is the equipment I asked you to prepare ready to go?"

"Yes sir," replied Raven with a very serious look on his face accentuating the scar on his left cheek.

"Good, now good luck and please send my regards to the master. Tell him that I'm a changed man now," smiled Vallentorvan.

Raven also returned a smile to him and then looked at Valkin and tapped him on his shoulder. "Alright Val, come along. We must make haste to Hallucagenia."

Valkin didn't ask any more questions of his masters. He was beginning to accept them as his masters. He didn't have much of a choice. They clothed him. They fed him. They practically kept him alive. Deep down in his core being, he was very thankful for that. However, forever on his mind was the thought of being re-united with his mother and he was prepared to do whatever it takes to get back to her, even if it meant fighting a war he never knew was being waged and he never dreamed he would be a part of.

They stepped outside amidst a flurry of activity. Barbarian foot soldiers from Hallucagenia in the southwest were just arriving fully clad with armor and axes ready for an impending battle. Raven was walking hurriedly through the rabble trying to get somewhere but Valkin was not sure where just yet and so he asked the question that was on his mind,

"Raven, do you think those dragons and snakes are coming back today."

"I don't little brother, maybe, maybe not! Either way, we're not taking any chances. These people need our protection and we are going to do our best to give them that."

Finally, the two warriors reached the circle in the middle of a group of white battle camp tents, and there standing proudly were Pixie and Mike all saddled up and ready to go.

"Hi, Raven, and Valkin, so nice to see you."

"Nice to see you too, Pixie. How's Rufor?" asked Valkin as Mike gave a low chuckle in the background. Valkin smiled as Raven strapped up the two wolves.

"Fine, I'm sure," replied Pixe in a very sarcastic manner. "I see his influence upon you hasn't left. Mike, you have such a big snout which I'm going to bite off hard one day."

"Oh baby wolf, you can bite me anytime," smirked Mike.

Pixie was about to charge at him when Raven cut in breaking up the fight.

"That's enough you two! We have a very important mission. We are to escort Valkin to the island of Gilipriel. Now focus, and stay sharp, you know what the journey entails. Don't falter." Raven jumped onto Pixie as Mike gulped hard.

"What's wrong Mike, the cat caught your tongue?" asked Pixie seeing the visible discomfort upon the dirty brown wolf's face.

"Never! I just don't like that place. It's beautiful but creepy at the same time. Hey Val, good luck buddy. Good luck buddy! You gonna need it!"

Valkin now had a look of concern upon his face at Mike's ill-omened declaration as he mounted him.

"Enough chit chat kids, let's move!"

Raven and Pixie were the first to speed off! Pixie's pinkish hue fluttered through the crowds as she sped towards the walls. When they finally caught up with Raven and Pixie, Valkin and Mike collectively jumped over the walls of Hallucagenia from the North side.

They traveled North West reaching the shores of Gilipriel within a few days camping under many solemn firelights. Raven didn't say much. He was a man of few words. Pixie and Mike were also unusually quiet, so much so that Valkin saw fit to ask Mike what was wrong.

"Oh, nothing's wrong Valkin. It's just the place we are going to! It's filled with strange things, strange creatures, and an old man they call, the master! It makes me fell uneasy."

Valkin was curious and wanted to know more.

They waited for Raven to go off to sleep and then they talked more about the master.

"They say he trained the Death Brothers but even before that, he was involved in training the Dark Knights too."

"WHAAT! The Dark Knights, like Tereartre!" gasped Valkin. "Those entities that Melody and Tereartre transform into when they want to specifically kill people quickly. Why encourage that?"

"A fair question! What I heard was that he taught them how to control their awesome power. You see many moons ago, your..." Mike was interrupted unexpectedly by the dark figure of Raven appearing out of nowhere. He had a beady look in his orange eyes.

"I believe it's your turn to take watch, Mike."

"Yes sir." Mike immediately got up from his crouched position and walked out of the camp area to do his rounds. He twitched his snout with some irritation feeling robbed.

Raven went back to his place as Pixie returned from her rounds to fall asleep next to Raven.

Valkin crept back and put his hands behind his head and looked at the stars. He wondered about what Mike was going to tell him. With those thoughts in mind, he went into a deep sleep.

The next day brought the four warriors closer to their intended destination as they arrived on the pristine, idyllic shores of the Galapaluan island chain system.

Gilipriel was an uninhabited island separated from the mainland and the main islands of the Galapalaun island chain and the rest of the vast ocean. The distance between the mainland and this island was only about 546 yards. The Gilipriel shoreline was a golden brown in the morning sunlight and shimmered a brilliant, peaceful white at midday and pale blue in the moonlight at night. It was quite beautiful indeed. All it lacked was a glass of freshly-made juice and a leaf umbrella to complete the picture-perfect portrait of an ideal place to retire. Across the horizon to its right was another small island that rose from the sea into a mountain with subtle juniper green trees and lanky palms at her front base. Many birds flew around its peninsula making strange gurgling noises. It was clear that they were some sort of White Sea gulls.

The warriors marveled at the site before them, which was gently perturbed by the presence of a small boat that rustled against shores twisting and turning as it washed up now and again. It seemed to be an invitation to the warriors. Valkin was enticed to hop into the boat but when his fellow companions completely ignored it, he chose to follow suit.

"Our path leads up the Gregor mountains," replied Raven.

They traveled up a Gregor mountain pass for many hours until finally they reached the summit. Valkin, who reached the pinnacle first, was awarded the first gaze of the island that was going to be his home for the next couple of days. He looked at the Island where he was going to be spending most of his time. It looked quite a distance away and there was no boat in sight but for the one that was left behind. He looked back to see if it was still there only to find that it was gone. It had completely vanished.

"Hey guys, where's the boat gone?"

"You'll see!" remarked Raven smiling at Valkin.

Valkin resolved that he would probably have to swim for it after they traversed the other side of Gregor Mountain. The sea was calm enough. Only a few small waves were coming in, nothing major. Throughout their journey to the Galapalauan shores, not many words were mentioned and not many questions were asked by Valkin to Raven. Deep down, he knew that what he was going to be put through was of great importance and he felt that any question he wished to ask would be better answered by experience.

Raven then rode in front of Valkin and disembarked from Pixie.

"This is as far as I go with you, Valkin. Instruction was given to me to stay on the shoreline and protect you from any outside dangers that you may encounter if our enemies get wind of your whereabouts."

"Now, I have to ask a question, Raven. Who cares if I get taken by them? Why am I here?"

"We do. You mean something to us. You mean something to yourself and to the people you love and care about. All of this is not for nothing! For all they know, this could be a ploy to throw them off. You will find out why you are here soon enough!"

Valkin looked at Raven and contemplated the meaning of his last words. Could it mean that he wasn't part of any grand plan, that they were just using him for misdirection to throw King Braithwaite and his allies off from their real threats? Whatever the reason was, Valkin felt pretty useless at that particular moment. "I will say no more. Let's see how things pan out."

"Okay fine! I have another question, Raven. How am I going to get across to the island? Do I have to swim across or is there another boat because the one we left behind is no longer there?"

"Neither, you could probably try it but the shoal of sharks that protect the island would probably get you first like how they got the boat first."

"Come on Raven, you're bluffing! Sharks, protecting an island, you've got to be kidding me. Sharks don't come to the shoreline, do they? They sell them on fish markets dead and dusted. I thought they were no more sharks in open waters anymore?"

"Clearly, you have not been to the ocean recently, Valkin," replied Raven with cynicism in his voice. "It's true what you say to an extent. There aren't many left in the wilds, except for this place, Valkin. This is their last refuge from the exploitation of humans and other kinds," replied Raven clenching his fists.

"I've never actually seen a wild shark before. I've never actually been to the sea before. This is all strange and wonderful for me. I wonder what kind of temperament they have," replied a very clueless Valkin.

"You'll soon find out…" smiled Raven.

Valkin smiled back.

They shook hands and Valkin approached the waters that swished and swirled on the shoreline.

Mike shook his head readying himself. "HOLD ON, VALKIN, HERE WE GO!" Mike grabbed onto Valkin gently by the waist of his black assassin uniform provided by the Death Brothers hoisting Valkin upon his back and ran towards the shoreline at an incredibly fast pace. Just before Mike's legs could hit the water breaking on the shores, he leaped up high into the sky.

Valkin looked below and saw giant rocks moving in the water. They were huge, about 100 ft in length and 16 ft in width. Valkin thought to himself what those rocks could be. They couldn't be rocks though, he thought because rocks don't move and then, he looked more closely seeing one of the rocks surfacing from beneath the waves revealing the largest-looking dorsal fin he'd ever seen in his life. Then only, did Valkin realize that they were bloody super sharks, all ten of them he could count circling the Island, always alert, and always on the prowl for food. Valkin saw pockets of blood-stained spurts of water here and there indicating a recent kill, no doubt. He then turned his head to focus on the Island that they were fast approaching.

It was a fairly large island, lush and green, and very mountainous as well.

Mike and Valkin were now descending onto the shoreline. Mike widened out his paws, slowing their descent, and prepared for landing. They hit the ground hard, which was expected, but what was unexpected was Valkin hitting the ground hard as well. Luckily, they had landed on the softer bed of sea sand. Valkin's head and hands were buried in the sand and his legs were waving around widely because he couldn't breathe. Mike helped a sneezing and coughing Valkin out of the sand. Valkin wiped his face and dusted his brownish hair which was littered with sand particles and shells. Mike laughed at him. It was amazing how similar in appearance Mike and Rufor were. In fact, one could almost not tell them apart. What delineated them was their fur colors.

Valkin shook his head. "Damn! What happened, Mike?"

"Sorry Val, guess I hit the ground a little too hard back there!"

"Don't worry about it. I'm still alive, unfortunately," remarked Valkin as he hit Mike's stomach. "Look at this place Mike. It's a paradise. Let's explore a bit, and see if we can find the master."

"I've got a feeling that he'll find us," smiled Mike.

Valkin and Mike then made their way toward the dancing palm trees that lined the shoreline of Gilipriel island.

The palm trees then gave way to a lusher jungle environment with larger vegetation and forest canopies. Birds with twelve wings chirped and whistled away above. It was the strangest sight that Valkin experienced. Little creatures scurried here and there taking cover from the intruders that were invading their undisturbed and wild space.

Valkin and Mike then came to the foothills of a rockface. It wasn't very large, about 218 yards in height but vast in terms of its breadth. It would take at least half a day's journey to travel around the mountain face, so they decided to traverse the cliff face. It was jagged, indicating good handholds and many potential routes to climb.

"Hey Mike, you better stay behind just in case I fall."

"Fuck no! I'm not staying behind, not in this place. I can climb a fucking mountain. Perhaps, even better than a human like yourself."

"It's a long way up, Mike. I don't want you to strain yourself and break a claw or worse," replied Valkin desperately fighting his laughter back.

"Ha ha! Very funny, short man! In that case, would you rather let me stand aside and let you hit the ground hard when you fall, Valkin, because I can do that?" replied Mike with a smile on his face.

"No, I wouldn't want that. Oh, come on then." Mike and Valkin had a chuckle and then Valkin started his ascent up the rockface.

They started their arduous climb and found that the rock wasn't actually rock. It was hard mud, sunbaked by the early morning rays. At the base of the mountain, it cracked exposing its softer inner layers that Valkin and Mike found themselves sometimes sinking in. As they ascended, the mud had become seemingly more solid and sturdier making it easier to ascend the sheer cliff faces. Mike found the appearance of the mountain rather strange as he climbed.

They eventually got to the halfway point to some curled dead tree stumps that stuck out from the rock face as giant toothpicks. They decided this was where they will rest for a short time to regain their strength and breath. Valkin and Mike perched themselves upon the ailing tree stumps and admired the view from where they sat for a few moments after which they decided that they must press on to their destination. Valkin stood up first and felt the tree branch that he was standing upon slowly rise upwards. The dry, sunbaked mud around it began to flake and crack releasing large chunks of debris below its shaky roots. Mike and Valkin were stunned with confusion as to what was going on. Then, without warning, the tree stump lifted suddenly sending Valkin hurtling high into the air, luckily towards the mountain itself. Valkin had to react quickly and grabbed ahold of the closest grip he could find when he eventually came to a halt in midair. He looked below him and saw that Mike was still there and shouted to him,

"WHAT'S GOING ON!"

"AVALANCHE VAL, KEEP MOVING UP, I'M RIGHT BEHIND YOU!" Mike jumped from his tree stump just as it suddenly moved upwards and suddenly realized that he was gravely mistaken.

It was not an avalanche that was bringing down the mountain! In fact, it wasn't a mountain at all. It was one of the local monsters! The tree stumps were its eyelashes opening to reveal a blue-green eyeball with a fiery orange pupil in the center large enough to resemble a small pond.

Valkin and Mike had no time to think about what they were climbing upon as the creature released itself from the ground from where it was basking in the sun until roused from its slumber by the two strangers.

The torso of the creature was broad and now Valkin and Mike were fast approaching its spine crossing over it to the other side but their view of the land became distorted as the creature rose and stood upon its hind legs. It let out a hissing screech and followed that up with a roar as it turned to its left making its way to the water. Valkin and Mike soon realized this and decided that the ride they got upon the creature, not to mention waking it up, was a testament to the overstaying of their welcome and decided to disembark. They jumped off the side of the creature, first Mike, then Valkin. Mike touched the ground first, allowing his massively powerful paws to act like shock absorbers like the prowess of his cat cousins. Valkin followed soon after as the creature's tail swung around to him. He quickly rolled along the rugged ridge further breaking his fall and allowed Mike to jump up to catch him midair before they sped off in the opposite direction to where the creature was going. From afar, the creature was the most placid one they had seen thus far. They surmised that it could have been a herbivore. It eventually made its way to the ocean and disappeared beneath the gentle waves leaving behind a great void in the land allowing the midday sunlight to once again penetrate through the jungles of Galapalau.

Valkin and Mike were still breathing heavily with muddy sweat dripping from their bodies reeling from the shock of actually surviving their ordeal. Mike looked at Valkin and began to laugh and so did Valkin. They laughed for a few minutes as they fell to the ground in complete and utter exhaustion after their terrible ordeal.

Suddenly, Valkin got up first smelling a faint whiff of smoke in the air. "Do you smell that Mike?"

"Yes, I do. That is definitely smoke and where there's smoke, there's fire."

They scanned their horizons and could see some smoke rising from the other shore on the other side of the island. It was midday now and the day was young. Mike estimated that it was about two hours walk away from where they were currently standing. They were on track planning to be where the smoke originated from just before nightfall.

The going was slow however mainly due to the dense undergrowth but the smoke signals were getting stronger and closer as they bellowed and puffed into the air. An hour had passed and Mike and Valkin decided to take another apprehensive break on the grass within the dense undergrowth. Valkin pulled out a tuft of grass and squeezed the moisture out of it into Mike's mouth to quench his thirst and then into his. The day was quite warm but the shade of the trees kept them cool in the humid environment. They decided to take a nap to recuperate and gather their strength. Valkin lied down on Mike's stomach and fell off to sleep. Mike kept one eye open but also eventually fell off into deep slumber too. After half an hour of sleep, a deep hissing bellow woke them up gradually. Valkin pulled out his blue and white sword from the sheath attached to his waist and prepared for whatever was making that ill sound. Mike looked around growling softly, covering Valkin's frontward scan of the environment.

Suddenly, the trees gave way in front of them driving them backward with surprise revealing the largest lizard they had ever seen. Mike and Valkin stepped further back to give the hissing behemoth some room to move around fearing that the lack thereof would enrage it further. They were afraid and the giant lizard could see it in their eyes. It's forked tongue flicked in an out of its mouth. Its orange eyes were fixed on both

Mike and Valkin as it drooled sticky venomous saliva mixed with blood and who knows what else. It kept on shifting its head from side to side focusing on the intruders that were invading its humble abode. Its sharp curved teeth were primed as it snapped its snout at them repeatedly hissing loudly as it did. Valkin's heart was racing as he held his sword tightly with both his trembling hands. Mike was crouched low ready to attack the beast. The leathery skin of the 40 ft long lizard was hard and poised for a kill.

Valkin quietly spoke out, "Hey Mike…" whispered Valkin "…what is that thing?"

"That Valkin, is a Komodracon, one of the deadliest Island creatures, there is. Be on your guard, this isn't the placid monster we encountered earlier," whispered Mike.

Valkin was tense readying himself for an eminent attack. "Wonder if it's the same size as those sharks in the ocean?" asked Valkin still mesmerized by the sheer size of this scary creature.

"Most definitely and it has killed many as well, young man! Isn't that right Zeldor?" replied an old man who suddenly appeared from the bushy undergrowth behind the lizard which now became completely tame in his presence.

The old man wore an orange shawl draped around his thin 4.5 ft, 88 lb body. He wore no shoes, which allowed his feet to take on an earthly brown complexion. They seemed more blackened with many barefoot steps taken all around his island paradise home and looked burnt with hardiness. He walked up to Zeldor and petted the lizard's head and for a moment it actually looked like a tame wolf. It smiled and stuck out its forked tongue in friendliness.

Valkin sheathed his sword and Mike let up his defensive posture in awe as he had never heard of a Komodracon tamed to such an extent.

The old man walked closer to Mike with his crooked branch fashioned into a walking stick. His wrinkled face and frizzy white hair made the old man look very old and wise indeed. The old man's voice was deep but soft and clear. "My Gosh, look at you little Mike. You don't remember me, do you?"

Mike scratched his head a bit thinking hard about whether or not he should remember the old man.

"The last time I saw all of you, was when you were mere pups. My word, how much you have grown! How is Pixie, is she here as well? And what about Rufor your brother, how is he doing? Please send him my regards when you see him. I will tell your father and mother how proud they should be of you."

The lizard behind the old man then lied down but kept its head high and was still very alert, looking on and keeping very still, focusing on Valkin and Mike.

"Yes, Pixie is here with Raven," replied Mike with a relieved look on his face searching his memory banks trying to place the old man within them.

"My Gosh, Raven. He must be a young man now?" asked the old man walking closer and closer to Mike.

"Yes sir, he is," replied Mike. Valkin was growing suspicious sensing something was amiss.

"...and how is Marve? He must be grown up to?" The old man was 6 ft away from Mike and as he came closer to stroke Mike's head, Mike started to feel very sleepy.

"Yes, he'ss!!!! Yeszzzz!!! He'zzzz!............" Mike began to slur and then he couldn't answer at all as he slowly fell to the ground losing consciousness. His neck began to droop down as his body felt limp and keeled to one side.

Valkin creased his eyebrows sensing something strange was going on and he slowly reached for his sword but only held the handle for now not drawing it. Valkin was helpless and couldn't stop what was happening to Mike. However, he felt that he could catch the old man off his guard with a surprise attack.

The old man closed his grey, clear eyes and held the stub of his walking stick whilst Zeldor stood up and came forward gently snuggling its head underneath Mike's body and whisking him away into the forest in a flash, disappearing into the lush vegetation in a matter of a few seconds. The old man looked ahead in Valkin's direction but with his eyes closed and a look of bliss upon his face. Valkin was already behind him pointing his sword at the old man's head firmly.

The old man was two feet shorter than Valkin. He was bordering on dwarfism. The old man smiled!

129

Valkin was about to slash the old man in half when the old man turned around only to be holding Valkin's sword in his left hand tapping the hilt with his right.

Valkin looked at his bare hands wondering when and how he was relieved from his sword.

"Such an exquisite sword you have here boy! Filled with history and memory and not to mention, great power!"

Valkin began to shiver a bit as he backtracked away from the old man slowly and carefully with a look of horror upon his face. The temperature outside was very hot but he shivered nonetheless.

The old man leaned on the sword burying it into the ground. "Such a violent world we live in hey! We have no need for your sword now, maybe when we can learn to use it to find peace, perhaps we will resurrect it from the earth that safeguards it." Within a few seconds, the sword was buried in the ground. Out of sight and out of mind so to speak! Valkin then only realized who the old man could be. The old man was the master!

"It was the master, himself," thought Valkin. A mixture of fear and wonder overcame him stunning him and making him immobile.

"Do you fear me boy?" asked the old man.

Valkin could not speak. He was speechless!

The old man walked up to Valkin and smiled and looked up to him.

"You remind me so much of your father. It's like peering through a windowpane into the past. It is humbling and nostalgic to have you here, Valkin Kendor, son of Helleus Kendor." The old man then turned around and walked away leaving Valkin behind. "Come! Let us walk along the shore and talk."

Valkin suddenly snapped out of his trance-like state and followed the old man towards a clearing through the forest revealing a beautiful shoreline just like the one they came from.

"Don't worry about Mike. It's my way of telling someone to give us some privacy, unobtrusively and without incident. He will meet us again tomorrow after he has rested. I understand the mountain giant of Gregor greeted you two earlier on?"

"We are grateful to have survived our encounter, Master," replied Valkin as he bowed forward in respect.

The two started their walk along the shoreline. Valkin kept a sidewards gaze on the old man at all times taking care never to stray his attention for fear of also being caught in the old man's sleeping trap. The old man was the first to break the awkward silence between them.

"Relax Valkin, don't look so worried. I won't hurt you nor will I put you off to sleep permanently, haha!"

Valkin turned to face the old man with a look of surprise upon his face.

"There it is again. Telepathy!" thought Valkin. He had encountered this strange and amazing ability before most strongly in Vallentor and Tereartre Levon at the outset of his journey and now, here it was again.

The old man continued, "I sensed a great disturbance within you Valkin, the moment you arrived upon the island. What plagues your mind at such a young age?"

"Firstly, I know and feel that you are the master but how can I be really sure?" asked Valkin feeling he needed to know if he was really speaking to the master before continuing.

"A fair question! Well, close your eyes for a moment then."

Valkin obeyed the old man's command and initially saw nothing in his mind's eye but darkness. This continued for a few seconds. Then, a picture started to develop. It was a picture of the island. He was then taken on a journey around the island in a few seconds, transported to every little nook and cranny there was revealing no-one else and coming back to his present position. Valkin then slowly opened his eyes.

The old man smiled and looked at Valkin. "Valkin, that was no illusion, if that's what you're thinking. There is no-one else here but us. Come, speak your mind to me, son. I may be able to help you."

Somehow, Valkin felt that Vallentorvan wouldn't send him to a wizard in order to manipulate his mind. Valkin felt that this old man was no lier and had a look of sincerity and authenticity in his old grey eyes.

"I believe you, Master. But who am I, old man? I mean, people keep bantering my father's name to me, like I'm supposed to think that it means something. I never knew the man! I was born. There was m mother and my grandfather and that was all the family I knew and had. What is my purpose on this island and in this war? Is it fate that controls my mind and blows it away with the wind? I'm not quite sure what is really going on. I feel like that lost boat drifting aimlessly in a lonely shoreline waiting to be gobbled up by the sharks," asked a very worried Valkin.

"Who do you think you are, Valkin?" asked the old man.

"I am a simple farm boy from Tillmandor," replied Valkin.

"Mmm ok. That's your truth but the world is much bigger than Tillmandor and so is your family. No Valkin! You are not a simple farm boy. You are much more! Perhaps, you need to stop fighting the current and get yourself a paddle to row with, and then you can control the direction you wish to go towards and avoid being eaten by the sharks. What do you think is your purpose in war?"

"I am here with the barbarians to defeat King Braithwaite but I wish I knew what part I play in this story, old man! As you said, I don't have a paddle to row with. Even if I did, I wouldn't know which direction to paddle towards. Deep down, I feel that there must be something more to this predicament."

"There always is, boy. And your purpose in this war is to find peace! What controls your mind and affects it so much?" The old man put his hands around his back and clasped them. His walking stick hovered behind him.

Valkin was completely unaware of it.

"Something that I cannot describe but I know it's there, old man, deep within me. Do you sense it?"

"Yes, Valkin, I do. It is a man with no identity, no purpose, and no control over himself. A man with something else as well. Very interesting! Why live then? Why prolong the inevitable?"

Valkin was taken aback by the suggestion made by the old man and actually considered it for a moment.

"Are you considering your own death, boy?"

Valkin looked at the old man again with surprise.

"Do you know what we are, Valkin?"

"No old man," replied Valkin with a bit of guilt on his face.

"We are, what we think and feel we are! We are sometimes what others make us out to be and sometimes, what we are what we make ourselves out to be. It is not only our minds that play a role in our lives. Our body and soul have a role to play as well. If the body is hurting, then the mind is fooled into weakness but it is the body that is hurting not the mind. Just like that, if the soul is afflicted, it will reveal its condition in the mind. Do you understand this concept, Valkin?" The old man talked slowly but with impeccable clarity in a slow-paced wisened voice that rang true deep within Valkin's conscious.

"For the most part, I do!"

"Good, I have watched over you for many years now, Valkin. Rolling on the ground, punching walls, and wallowing in your sorrow whilst trying to burn the clothes of your rage and inability to control your actions nor help yourself. I have seen the guilt and waywardness of your life. I am here to guide you to give yourself some direction."

Valkin felt as if the old man had peered deep into his very soul revealing everything about himself. He dropped his head slightly in shame.

"You wish to change without accepting the changes that need to be made. You wish to become something or someone you are not all the time yet you don't want to be just yourself. You draw strength from others but not from yourself. Your hypocrisy has been stressful and taxing leaving you with only small shreds of identity and purpose. It seems that every day, small bits of you fall off, revealing your true lies."

Valkin sniffed and allowed a tear to fall on his right cheek.

"Cheer up Valkin! This is not the end. On the contrary, it is only the beginning for you. You were sent here to me for a purpose and that is to give you back your purpose."

"Can you help me, old man!" pleaded Valkin.

"The only way I can help you is if you are willing to help yourself, boy. How badly do you want to change in your life? No-one else is afflicted around you. You have become a prisoner of your thoughts. Now is the time to free yourself and your mind. This is an island! There are only four of us here. You are isolated and so we shall isolate the problems within you and deal with them together. Now you feel and I shall speak as you feel, Valkin. Close your eyes and let us walk along the shore and reflect upon your life."

Valkin closed his eyes and began to think long and hard about all the things that worried him. Then, he felt a hard, wrinkled hand hit the back of his head. Valkin opened his eyes. He rubbed his sore head.

"Feel Valkin, feel with your mind. Don't force your thoughts. Let them flow."

Valkin then closed his eyes once again and began to feel as the old man commanded.

"Ahh! You see problems arise when they materialize when they are given the problem status when they overwhelm you. Every problem you have encountered, you have created, Valkin. Managing and dealing with problems created is the answer to all problems for it is the definition that must be changed in your mind for it to change in your life. Then, you will realize that there is no problem. It's all an illusion. Look again, Valkin. See how much time and energy you've spent concentrating on the darkest moments of your life. The lighter parts have been so clouded and some have even been all but forgotten. What a pity! All are memories of a time. That would be a big surprise for you to believe that they once existed. So, you've accepted the challenges that you present to yourself. That is good for it is the first step towards greater things. Do you know there are periods in your life where you actually forget about the things that plagued you?"

Valkin was about to open his eyes in recognition of the old man's observations but was cut short.

"I didn't say you must open your eyes, so let us continue."

Valkin took in a breath of fresh air and continued.

"Yes, look at that, a period where you were free from any sort of misery. Have you ever wondered what was different between that period and now, Valkin? You can open your eyes now."

Both Valkin and the old man stopped behind a palm tree.

Valkin opened his eyes. "I had less to think about it."

"True! But what exactly did you think about less."

"My problems, I guess."

"Yes, that is correct. You had fewer problems to think about. If you were thinking about the ocean in front of you, then this small palm tree will not affect your view, right? Only if you stand behind it and try and view the sea, will it obscure your view. I have said that we allow many things to affect our wonderful view of this world. We are so caught up with our blunders that we forget to bask in this beauty that is all around us. Therein lies your solution. You were not made to imitate others. You were made to learn from them for they too have made many mistakes in their lives. You were put here in this world to learn how to be yourself. Sometimes, we need to forget. We need to free the space within our

134

minds to store better things in the cubicles of our minds. We need to do this periodically or our minds may become overrun with unnecessary clutter. You are wondering about the body and soul. The mind or consciousness controls the body and the mind is a product of the soul, which cannot be quantified. So whatever level you choose to change, it will affect all the levels of your existence. There are more than just three levels of existence you know."

Valkin creased his eyebrows and wondered what the old man was alluding to.

"Do not worry about that for now, Valkin. For now, we know the body can do many things but still cannot succeed in changing the decisions made by the mind. Likewise, the mind can fool the soul and not allow the individual to truly live. What must we then change, Valkin? Is it our actions, our thoughts, or our spirit? You can only change what you think and believe you have the power to change. I can show you techniques to calm and still your mind but you may believe otherwise and it may not work. We can jump around wildly and learn the Dark Knightean martial arts and the power of the Spireneé[6] but it may not work for you. You decide what will work and what won't. Only you will know, Valkin. There is no secret formula for inner peace; no magical recipe that I can whip up for you in an empty coconut shell. There is only you and your desire for it. How it manifests is up to you alone. That brings us to the next point. Do you know what a master is Valkin?"

"No old man!"

"A master is not a master. Until one realizes that, then only does one become a true master of all one's faculties. Many so-called masters only retain the title because of others who believe in them, but the true master does not require belief from others; only the belief in oneself for believing only what others believe about oneself is folly. Naturally, a master is humbled by the attention received but never allows it to fuel an ego that does not exist within. Some so-called "masters" have great egos. But Valkin, you hold that majestic sword of yours to their throats and they'll do anything for you no matter how big their egos are!"

Valkin nodded in complete agreement and smiled at the old man's cheerfulness.

---

[6] Pronounced Spee-rin-nay

"Valkin, a master becomes a master usually when he has mastered a certain field or discipline. My field of specialization is specifically the Spireneé martial arts. They say when one becomes too involved in many fields where none get addressed with determination and undivided attention, then one cannot possibly expect to master any field. The mind constantly races. When it is still, certain things become clear! I am not telling you to concentrate only on one field at a time. I am telling you to put all your effort into whatever you are doing at that moment in time. That way, no-one can say you did not give it your best shot, right? A master always tries and never gives up. One can eventually ascend to the level of single mastery and become a multi-disciplinary master. I am a master of the Spireneé martial arts but also an excellent cook. Haha!"

Valkin and the master had a good laugh at the joke, which notably reduced the tension.

"Thus a master is not aware that he/she is a master. Others will be aware that you are. They will feel your presence and respect will not be commanded but earned. That's the idea, Valkin."

"So a master is humble."

"Everyone should be humble, Valkin. Humility is all around us. Nature is humility amplified. The water will flow and not be proud of it. It will just flow. The wind will blow and not be proud of it. It will just blow. Trees will grow without any pride even though the existences of many other animals depend on the survival of the trees and the flowing of the water and the gentle morning breeze."

The two continued their walk along the beach with the evening approaching. Valkin had his head down and looked at the sand he was going to trod on. The old man who was much shorter than him looked up at his new student and sighed.

"Valkin, that is not the answer!"

"I know but I wonder why so many have used it as the easy way out."

"That is true but it is also the hard way back in, right? Death for us is inevitable. That is a fact. However, an untimely death is a true tragedy! Acknowledge that you and I will not live forever and thus be free from the notion of death. It should not affect you, for you won't be here to be affected right? Think about the people you love and how they will feel when you leave them behind. Many don't think about life in that way and when it's too late, then only they realize the folly of their actions. Ever lost someone close to you Valkin?" asked the old man.

"Yes." A long pause followed after Valkin said who it was. "It was a family member, my grandfather."

"I'm very sorry to hear that, Valkin," sighed the old man rolling his lips.

"I got over it. He was a good man, always smiling and very cheerful. He had lived a full life. I miss him."

"Sometimes, Valkin, we need to celebrate the lives of the fallen and remember why we live. Do you still feel no purpose in your life?" asked the old man.

"Not anymore, but sometimes I feel worthless I must admit old man. That's how I feel. I feel like I should get beaten to a pulp and die within my pool of blood or sacrifice myself to save others."

"Why do you feel like that? Is it because of your defeat by the hands of Ordanian or is it your nature to be strong and hard on yourself?"

Valkin dropped his head slightly in acceptance that the old man's deductions about him were very accurate.

The old man noticed Valkin's gesture and pressed on. "Is it because you feel that you have sinned for the greater part of your life?" Valkin shed another tear. "You are not who you were Valkin, do you know that? You are who you are and who you are is who you will be."

Valkin's eyebrows creased because he couldn't understand what the old man was saying. He still felt he meant nothing to the world and no one. He wanted to be dead right then, right now. He wanted everyone else to be happy except himself. Then he realized something. He realized something a friend once told him many years ago when they were teenagers he didn't understand it then but now he finally understood what he was talking about. His friend said to him, "What if life is just a dream, what if we are all sleeping, and when we die we wake up to something else? What if there is no death, what if there is only eternity, this vast expanse of something that never ends? How must we live? What must we do? How should we love those around us? What is the way forward now?"

The old man shook his head and looked at Valkin. "You know Valkin, your friend was right! I don't know what lies beyond my end but do you think for one moment that I worry about it? I am too busy living instead of dying, Valkin."

Valkin took a deep breath in. "

Living Valkin, truly living and expressing yourself, your authentic self! Not following in the footsteps of others but forging new paths of your own which others can follow if they choose."

Valkin nodded in agreement and felt empowered. It was getting late and the sun was going down changing the blue skies into an opaque afternoon hazy orange curtain which fell over the glorious horizon.

"Valkin, before we retire for the evening, the time has finally come for you to be purged of your inner demons."

Valkin was taken aback by what the old man just said. Valkin's eyes widened in anticipation and intrigue!

"What is this old man talking about? Inner demons, what inner demons? Nobody told me about any inner demons. What's going on here?" thought Valkin.

"Yes, Valkin, your inner demons! There was one attempt in your life to purge them. It was successful but unfortunately, you have been infected again. It's about time we get rid of it. RIGHT NOW! It has been eating away at your very core. It has been suppressing your full development. It has been the root of your anger, your pain, and your suffering. It must go!"

"Master, please explain! What are you talking about? What demons? Nobody told me about any demons. I'm not possessed!" asked a very worried Valkin.

"The one within you, Valkin. You are not aware of it but it is hidden deep within your mind. It is very powerful as is your true strength. You will rise and go to the top but we need to get rid of the entity that is pulling you back down."

Suddenly, the old man lifted his hand releasing a massive amount of energy and light.

Valkin fell over and held his hands up blocking out the bright light that was clouding his vision.

The old man then shouted out, "AAROVALLAN![7]"

---

[7] Pronounced Ah-row-vaa-lan

Many miles away, the earth began to shake where the old man had buried Valkin's sword. The sword then burst its way out from beneath the ground and flew into the air straight into the hands of the old man trembling the earth around him with energy. His feeble-looking arms grasped the sword tightly and he pointed it at Valkin.

"COME A LITTLE CLOSER VALKIN," said the old man with a deep and powerful voice. "THIS WAS NOT SCHEDULED BUT IT MUST BE DONE. THIS WILL FEEL WEIRD BUT DO NOT BE AFRAID." The old man then thrust the sword into Valkin's belly and turned to release an incredible amount of energy from the boy.

Valkin screamed and shouted out with pain and discomfort feeling the blade of his sword swirl in his stomach. He then looked up. His eyes turned white and his teeth were becoming fangs. His brown hair got frizzy and blew wildly in the wind.

The master held the sword firmly and was determined to get rid of the emerging demon within Valkin. "BE GONE YOU & LEAVE THIS BOY ALONE!" he shouted.

"THE BOY IS MINE TO POSSESS. I HAVE DONE SO FOR MANY YEARS NOW AND WILL DO SO FOR MANY MORE!" Another voice was speaking through Valkin whose body was about to be ripped apart from the inside out. It seemed as if the demon was trying to manifest its true form by killing Valkin in the process. The cracks and fissures on the surface of Valkin's body made him look like a rock feature about to collapse.

"YOU WILL LEAVE HIM NICELY WITHOUT HARMING THE BOY," replied the old man turning the sword once more.

"NO, WHAT IS THIS? I KNOW THAT SWORD! IT IS THE SWORD OF LIGHT. NO-ONE CAN WIELD THE SWORD OF LIGHT BUT THE WIELDER HIMSELF AND HE IS DYING."

"DEMON, LOOK AGAIN!" The old man turned the sword once again and the demon cringed within Valkin and shouted out one last time and came out through the gaping wound made in Valkin's stomach. One could not see its true form. These entities don't have a form that mere mortals could see. Valkin fell into the sand and slipped into unconsciousness. The entire beach was dark and grey with a thick heaviness that slowly began to lift above the sunset.

The demon hovered above him. It was dark energy causing airwaves in the air.

"Help me, master, heal me and send me back for I have sinned greatly through this boy!"

"As you wish!" The master held up the sword and pointed it toward the demon who slowly disintegrated into thin air.

"Thank you, master. I did not mean to hurt anyone but I am at peace now. Thank you."

"Go well estranged soul." The old man bowed and walked over to Valkin and examined him. He smiled and hoisted him up on his little shoulder with ease and took him to his house.

The beach house and the awakening of

Valkin Kendor

"How do I override nature itself? What are your vices? How do you change a thought? It is said that one can change a thought with another more powerful thought. The answers are not always located outside yourself but sometimes within. We have to look deep within our core to find out who we truly are and what our purpose is in this wonderful world. I feel like for the greater part of my life I have been waging a war. I now want peace and love. I have mammoth tasks ahead of me but I feel tired and weary. I know I have the potential to do whatever I need to do. I just have to do it now. That's all. I'm a rebel to my own nature but I will not fight it anymore. I will merely change my being and become myself, which is an ongoing journey of discovery. The truth is within and without. Always running away, are we? Running away and into the war with no end. Lacerating yourself! I wish for peace in this world. There is too much pain and too much complaining. It really does make me sick. There are people who sleep on the floor every night. There are people who have nothing to eat every day and we worry about little things like how we look and the carriage we drive in. This and that! It makes me sick to feel that the life that was given to us is wasted on such mundane endeavors. You know what. I don't care about this anymore! I'm going to change things! I'm going to forge my own destiny. I will do it." Valkin's eyes were closed but his eyelids were fluttering wildly.

The master was next to him throughout his inner mental journey as Valkin slept on a wooden bed in a small house on the beach.

"Valkin, Valkin, wake up boy, wake up."

Valkin got up slowly and looked around to hear the ocean and waves breaking on the shoreline. He was in the simple hut of the master; nothing fancy, just some straw and wooden support beams to uphold the structure. The master was gentle and gently shook Valkin's back. "How was your journey? Did you find what you were looking for?"

"Yes, master. Through the dark clouds, a ray of sunshine shone through like a guiding light. For a long time, I have never felt such peace. Thank you!"

"I am very happy to hear that you're back with us Valkin. You still have much to learn but you are on the right road now. And what about this Princess I've heard so much about?" asked the master with a huge smile on his face.

"Nothing escapes your ears, does it master? Well, it's a strange relationship that we have, if you can call it a relationship at all. She tried to kill us, specifically me! She's an assassin but the strange decision for me was why did Vallentor send me and Rufor to save her. That doesn't make sense to me at all! I guess I feel pity for her and even if it got to a stage where we actually started to have feelings for each other, I don't want to be the one to hurt her, besides I'm way past my sell-by date anyway."

"Haha! Age is but a number, boy. You're surrounded by players whose morals are ten thousand times more warped and distorted than your own, Valkin and you say you're past your sell-by date. Boy, I think your friends if you have any left, went off meaning spoilt like spoiled food a long time ago. Nonetheless, it's quite a concern that she tried to assassinate you and Vallentor." Both Valkin and the master had a brief moment of contemplation. "Valkin, you're a true worrier." Valkin felt a little guilty. "You think too much. You worry too much. You're not living your wonderful life. Don't worry about that girl. Who's to say you'll even finish off with her in the first place." Valkin smiled. "You're wondering why I brought her up. Well, in my experience many a warrior has wavered in thought and action when a girl gets involved with him. I speak from experience by the way and let me tell you the outcome is always the same, disappointment. But, let's cross that bridge when you get there, boy, and then let's see how you handle things. And finally, let us train your mind, body, and spirit Valkin."

Valkin smiled and jumped off the bed looking out through the master's doorway filled with the morning sunshine. He stretched and flexed his muscles.

The master walked outside saying, "Follow me," to Valkin.

The Fall of Volcanock

"WHAT!" replied Vallentorvan with a look of disbelief and horror upon his face. "Are you sure, Rufor?"

"Yes good king, confirmed this morning. The city is completely destroyed, reduced to rubble! Not an ashblock on site! They took it all away and didn't leave much behind, just a few pieces were scattered here and there."

"Any survivors from the attack?" asked Tereartre with a look of concern and sadness on his face.

"Actually, there were no fatalities. All are well, but destitute for now. They are making their way to the Black Forests at the edge of the western borders of Hallucagenia in search of shelter and refuge."

Tereartre looked at Vallentorvan who was sitting on the resting chair in the meeting room contemplating what had just happened. Rufor looked at Vallentorvan and asked, "What do you think sir?"

"No doubt the work of the dragons of Razortor. Only they could traverse the length and breadth of the Wastelands of Selardor and come out unscathed with that amount of ashblock, but for what purpose? They must have flown over the storms, landed, taken a breather, and then destroyed the city," replied a speculative Vallentorvan. "They rode the dragons close to our boundaries along the North wall and picked up whatever they needed and returned to Sarcodia, but that is not what I'm concerned about. I'm really concerned for all those people. They are refugees of war wandering the Black Forests. We nearly died in there with our encounter with the giants. Where will they stay now? For all we know, Braithwaite's probably bartering ashblock or something to fund whatever campaign he's pushing but this time he's gone a bit too far! Never mind there were no fatalities. He's done something far worse. What kind of quality of life will those people lead now that they are refugees," contemplated Vallentorvan with his right hand holding his chin. He then stood up. "This tactic of his is low and dirty but we will respond to it appropriately."

"Perhaps, we should not be too hasty in our response," suggested Tereartre.

Vallentorvan looked towards Tereartre Levon who was staring deep into the fire. "We will not be able to launch any attack from the outside. Braithwaite is in the final phase of his plan. He is almost ready for war."

"I'm not talking about preparing for an attack, Tereartre. I'm talking about providing temporary shelter for King Brovinus and the people of Volcanock," replied Vallentorvan.

"He's diverted our attention sir so he can accomplish something even more sinister, Vallentorvan. Can't you see that?" replied a concerned Tereartre.

"I know, but nonetheless, our top priority is to accommodate those people even if we have to set up refugee camps in the battlegrounds. I don't care. Tereartre, Rufor, take a hundred barbarians with you to where the Minotaurs are located and give them this message. Bring them from the west side of Hallucagenia. Don't take them anywhere near DallaVega, please! Kindly brief the inner core of Hallucagenia that they'll be having visitors over for supper. They won't mind. We are a kind race."

Marve and Raven smiled at Vallentorvan's altruistic decision whilst a look of uneasiness prevailed over Tereartre and Rufor's faces only withheld by their strong resolves.

Tereartre though could not hold back his apprehension any longer. "I believe you are making a grave mistake Desire. There are limits to the barbarian's charity which you may not fully understand. If you bring the Minotaurs here, knowing the history between the two races, you will risk starting another war." Tereartre walked up to Vallentorvan and placed his hand upon his shoulders in a pleading manner, "This is a mistake. Do not do this. It is just too risky."

"Well Tereartre, what you ask for is a change of the very nature that makes Vallentorvan who he is from being magnanimous to being downright selfish, which quite frankly is very difficult for me to do. You know Tereartre, I served on the Latarial council and was robbed of my ideal for peace and harmony when the split kingdom's suggestion was proposed and finally accepted. What ensued afterward was a tragedy! All those lives were taken without an ounce of regret. Was it worth it in the end? I don't think so. All the people wanted was peace. I knew the likes of the rulers of the new split kingdoms and I knew that their philosophies would bring ruin to the lands. A civil war was inevitable and it seems that my prophesy is coming to pass! I must tell you that it is very difficult to bore the images of war out of our minds. I know you'll agree with me. We are going back to a dictatorship like the days of old, only this time the means and intentions behind it are far more evil and selfish, unlike the magnanimous rule of Selardor. There could have been an alternative to this but these are the kind of people we have to deal with now. These are the enemies of our day and age. Meeting the barbarians and living with them, experiencing such coexistence and respect turned me around and molded me into a better person. I hope we can perpetuate this way of being to the other more powerful figures of our time. In light of this, my first step towards realizing that ideal is to provide shelter for these refugees despite our bitter history. Your concerns have been duly noted Tereartre but my decision is final!"

Tereartre swallowed hard and tilted his head back and then bowed accepting Vallentorvan's difficult decision.

"We men have many terrible vices, Desire!" replied Tereartre.

"Yes we do old friend, but it is up to us to control those vices and channel our energy into a more positive direction. What is the need for such powerful vices when one can just rechannel the energy spent into another pathway?"

"Yes, but try telling that to King Braithwaite," replied Rufor standing up and walking past Vallentorvan to cuddle up closer to the fire taking comfort in the warmth of the room.

"Perhaps, I should. Braithwaite is no different from us when we were at that stage in our thinking, right warriors?"

"You are right!" replied Tereartre who sat down opposite Vallentorvan.

The firelight danced on the shiny triangular table top. "We train our bodies, mind, and spirit not for war but for the maintenance of peace."

"True, but what about the means for the maintenance of that peace, Tereartre? Those in search of peace can also be no different from the war-mongers exacting their mission using whatever means necessary to do so. The line between peacemaker and war-monger is very fine and needs to be distinguished."

"You make a good point Rufor. I have a solution for you. Take out the war factor; take out all forms of vices that intentionally or unintentionally hurt the mind or body. Take them all away and what are you left with? Peace, bliss, contentment, harmony, love, happiness, and so on. When there is no place for such negativity, the existing space is filled with all things positive. Are we in the clouds in terms of our thinking warriors?" replied Vallentorvan.

"I think so," replied Tereartre with a humble smile upon his face and a twinkle in his neon green eyes.

"Well, I think we are flying high and the rest of our fellow races should join the ride," suggested the King of Hallucagenia and DallaVega.

"I am a Dark Knight, sir. My path has been carved out in blood for me already. I get brief intermissions of peace in the Pine Forests. I wish that I could you in your flight of fancy, good king but alas someone has to fight," replied Tereartre with a straight face.

"Well, change it then Tereartre. You have such great power to do so. Change it, old friend! Get rid of the vice; liberate yourself and your mind. Become one with the cosmic tune of the universe and realize your true potential."

"Easier said than achieved, Desire," replied Tereartre looking back at the fire. Tereartre took in a deep breath and then stood up to leave. He opened the heavy wooden doors and just before walking through it he said, "All I know is that charity begins at home! Goodnight gentlemen." He walked away closing the doors behind him leaving Vallentorvan and the other warriors to contemplate their thoughts as they stared into the fire of the night.

Horses and wolves

The hatch to the underground rooms beneath the royal Sarcodian chambers flew open with the arrival of the foreboding King Braithwaite. His very presence struck fear into the magicians below who were working tirelessly for many years now, trying to perfect the creature they were commanded to create! They all worked a bit faster upon the arrival of his large figure descending the stairs. He climbed down wearing his long red, grey, and black Sarcodian royal robes. There seemed to be a mist in the air and a sticky dampness of sweat and perspiration along the walls and upon closer inspection, that was what it was. The underground chamber was situated just below the Sarcodian royal chamber. It was created many, many years ago and has survived since then. It's use is both wonderous and sinister. King Gilleus, who was talking to King Bellorus, was already underground awaiting the arrival of King Braithwaite. They were standing close to the underground balcony's edges overlooking the space below in which the magicians were doing their main research. There was very little light in the chamber itself, which was dimly lit by pale, green torches that lined the sides of the chamber. After King Braithwaite closed the main hatch leading to the chamber, even less light filtered in from above. All the magicians were skulking figures, old and weary with crooked wisdom and intellect far beyond that of any normal human man. They were everywhere. They lined the balcony with their clean white coats and hunched backs. They scurried from wooden bench-to-bench dissecting animal tissues of some kind as steam from boiling cauldrons vented into the stuffy atmosphere of the underground chamber. Strange lights from indescribable cupboards flickered on and off which the magicians were opening and closing releasing cold mist and retracting more tissues to test and dissect.

As King Braithwaite walked through the labyrinth, they made way for an approaching King Braithwaite bowing to him as he walked past. He had this sadistic smile upon his face and hands clasped behind his back finger tapping in the air with great anticipation in his cedar dark brown eyes. He stroked his beard now and then and rubbed his potbelly feeling full after his immense breakfast. Deep down, King Braithwaite felt that he was ready for some good news this morning as the magicians only send the news to the surface dwellers when they have breakthroughs in their efforts.

King Gilleus and Bellorus who were talking on the balcony overlooking the underground chamber joined King Braithwaite after briefly greeting him and followed closely behind him down the stairs to the lower level of the chamber.

King Gilleus had a straightface whilst King Bellorus could hardly contain his excitement. He was rubbing his old hands uncontrollably, shivering with excitement.

They looked over the balcony and admired the magicians who were scurrying around working, carrying papers and strange devices in their hands with flickering lights. The three kings then made their way down to the lower level. They used stairs made from steel that lined the wall. They reached the bottom floor and proceeded to walk right across it. King Braithwaite enjoyed the enthusiasm of the magicians and smiled at each one that bowed to him. Each one who crossed his path bowed and then quickly moved on.

"This way my lord," motioned King Bellorus suddenly taking the lead.

King Braithwaite was very impressed and wanted to know more about the facility. "Who are all these people, Bellorus, and where do you find them?"

A look of delight entered King Bellorus's settled ash-grey eyes as he rubbed his hands further. "They are the Magister of the Deviant Sciontouristé Society or DSS."

"Very interesting and who is their leader?" asked King Braithwaite.

"They called him Dioxyenatlas[8], the Dreadful!"

"Dioxyenatlas, never heard of him."

"Neither have I. Anyway, these are his minions. They are easily employed for a modest fee and accommodation. They work hard and deliver on their promises."

They reached the end of their walk at the very end of the bottom part of the chamber that was sealed off by ten large, steel meshes stacked behind one another for added strength cordoning off a large space ahead.

As King Braithwaite approached, he heard the strangest noises emanating from the mesh barrier. It was cold and slimy in this section of the chamber.

Then, he suddenly heard shouting from behind the enclosure. "HOLD IT, HOLD IT, RESTRAIN THE BEAST!"

The sounds intrigued him and he wanted to know what was going on below. What were those shouts about and why were those men making them? He could see some dim light and a rocky ceiling through the space but no more. He gathered that whatever the mesh was guarding further below needed to be guarded for a reason. The steel mesh overlooked an arena, the size of the Colosseum in Tillmandor, over a hundred yards in diameter.

King Braithwaite got closer and as he did, the noises became louder and he could start to see what was below.

It first sounded like those of a Bararg but softer mixed with the neighs of a horse that seem to be strangled and so the sounds that came out were high-pitched growls from the deepest darkest parts of the world.

King Gilleus wasn't happy at all when he got closer to the mesh and saw what was below.

King Bellorus hung back because he was genuinely scared of what lay beneath them but you could see that he was very excited.

King Braithwaite could not believe what he saw below!

---

[8] Pronounced Dee-ox-ee-en-at-las

The creatures were huge, slightly smaller than Barargs, but much more elegant and handsome. The trainers were dwarfed by the sheer size of them. Beautiful wolven paws, a horse's tail, and a broad horse's head with long spikey, furry coats like wolves all around their bodies. They ran around and were very playful sticking their tongues out and jumping from side to side. Their teeth were menacingly sharp but they drooled playfully as their masters played with them. Their rippling muscles bulged out as they ran around the entire circumference of the arena. Each had a mind of its own, but all were very disciplined and obeyed every command of their masters. In total, there were ten of them in the arena this time.

King Braithwaite smiled in satisfaction. The skulking figure of the chief magician in charge of the project then joined the three kings and marveled at the sight of his creatures, which he had a hand in creating. His nose was hooked and his face was filled with warts and wrinkled with age. He wore bright white robes and his hands were covered by their sleeves.

"May I brief King on the status of the creature?" asked the chief magician.

King Braithwaite turned around sharply and nodded his head.

"You have come at the right time, my Lord. The creatures you see before you have been now been perfected. The ashblock has been completely integrated into its exoskeleton. Allow me to demonstrate their unique abilities."

"Amazing, truly amazing! But before you do, what do you call these magnificent creatures?" asked King Braithwaite with awe and interest.

The magician smiled and replied, "They are called the 'Howls of Sarcodia', after your kingdom, my lord." The magician then shouted to one of the trainers in the arena.

He was not wearing a shirt, just brown trousers.

"NUMBER TEN. GO THROUGH THE EXERCISE!"

He nodded in affirmation and bowed to the creature before him. His creature was a full ink black with a lonely white patch on his chest and dark majestic locks of hair flowing over half of his broad face. All the creatures were very hairy and looked bulky but were very fast and agile.

The chief narrated further, "This particular creature's name is Ravenous and was christened the lord of all the Howls created. He was the tenth Howl of ten thousand created and surprisingly, he turned out to be the strongest of them all. However, we were not surprised as we used some of Rufor Rafelieus's blood to create him."

Ravenous began to give a piercing howl that shook the arena a bit. Then, he began to glow a white color as the ground below him attracted a substance to its body. It was ashblock!

King Braithwaite looked closely at the creature. He was intrigued by what he was witnessing. The Howl was being smothered in ashblock transforming into a rocky Howl. Once the process had ended after a few seconds, the Howl took on a new appearance. It retained its original colors but now it looked solid, like granite, impervious to any damage.

"Perhaps, a demonstration for my lord is in order?" enquired the skulking chief magician.

King Braithwaite agreed.

The trainer then took out his sharpest sword and axe and flung it square at the Howls head. The sword and axe left the trainer's hand with incredible force and speed but Ravenous just stood there unphased waiting to be hit in the head. Both the sword and axe hit his head and shattered to pieces upon impact. After that, Ravenous allowed his body armor to dissipate, as it was not needed anymore.

It brought a smile to King Braithwaite's face and the chief magician's.

King Gilleus swallowed hard whilst King Bellorus stood in shock and awe at what they had just witnessed.

King Braithwaite wanted to know more. "Speed?"

The chief magician looked up and replied, "faster than both a wolf and horse my lord."

King Braithwaite's eyes flickered with delight. He wanted to know more. "And strength and ferocity? What about intelligence? Can they speak?"

"We have not gaged their strength yet but they were engineered to be more civilized than both of the species that they were derived from and thus easier to control. In terms of speech, they have not yet uttered a word to us but we hear whispers after hours when they are left alone. They are indeed talking to each other! Our spies have revealed their intrigue about their very existence. They are more fascinated about themselves which ultimately is a good thing I believe."

"That is good. How will they fare against say a Dark Knight?" King Braithwaite turned around to face the chief magician suddenly and screamed releasing an incredible amount of energy. His eyes turned red and then they came on fire. His muscles contracted painfully revealing his true figure, which was far leaner and meaner than his current form.

Everyone moved away from him, except King Gilleus who stood right next to him firmly, seemingly unperturbed by his energy release.

King Braithwaite's robes eventually were burnt away revealing his well-built upper torso. He had fireproof pants specially made for him which he wore at all times. He did not attract any Dark Knightean armor to his body. He knew that someone would have died in the process. King Braithwaite then touched the iron mesh barrier in front of him. It melted immediately!

"GOOD KING!" shouted the chief magician with concern.

King Braithwaite just held up an arm saying that he was ok. He then jumped down into the arena hitting the earth with a loud thud forming a small crater around him.

The creatures sensed the presence of King Braithwaite's strength and became a bit edgy and restless retracting backward towards the shelter of their trainers.

The magicians were not too concerned as their trainers had full control over the creatures.

"Stand aside, trainer, and let me dance with your best. Ravenous, I hear you are very strong! Let us see how strong you are."

"So this is a Dark Knight that I've heard so much about. The Dark King of Sarcodia! I know that I am no match for you King but I will give you my very best, my very best," replied Ravenous in a deep voice in the common tongue to the magician's and trainers' surprise.

"They were scared to tell me that you are descended from *Higardo*[9], the legendary horse of Helleus Kendor! Am I not right? I could feel your presence the very moment I opened the chamber. I must admit that I was surprised and somewhat perturbed when the last remaining bloodline of Higardo was used to allow your creation. Perhaps, you should have

---

[9] Higardo was the name of the horse that Helleus Kendor rode into battle in the great barbarian war. Higardo was the lord of all horses.

remained a horse for austerity," replied King Braithwaite with a smile on his face.

"I am. It is true! However, I prefer to go by the name of Ravenous Rafelieus. Higardo is but a shadow of a memory in my dark past that runs only through my veins but I am far stronger now oh mighty King Braithwaite for the blood of the Rafelieus lineage also runs through me." Ravenous then howled as he attracted the immaculate ashblock armor and then he did something very unexpected. His eyes started to ooze fire as well and so did the fur on his feet and tail, very much like the flaming horse, Higardo, that Helleus presumably rode in with to Hallucagenia in his battle with Rehowlor the Lightning Elemental. He was truly marvelous to look at.

King Braithwaite smiled. "I expected nothing less than a fight to the death when I faced off against Higardo and I expect nothing less from you Ravenous. Let us dance!"

All the other creatures went to their trainers and stood with attention readying themselves to observe a true fight, their first fight. The air was thick with intensity and both warriors were poised for the kill. Such history lay between them! A feud that had been fuelled for many years now. Ravenous circled King Braithwaite who screamed again and tensed his body attracting the armor of the Dark Knights to himself now that he knew none of the valuable magicians would be hurt. The breastplate flew in from nowhere and smashed into one of the Howls and its trainer. Both landed awkwardly flat on the floor. The Howl just dusted itself up with two flicks of the head and got up shortly thereafter. Unfortunately, the trainer did not. The Howl, which was pure white, licked its trainer and nudged him, urging him to get up but its trainer did not respond.

King Braithwaite saw this and was very sad. He gritted his teeth and continued to attract the rest of his armor. Once all the armor pieces assembled upon Braithwaite's body, he walked up to the fallen trainer and stroked his Howl who reciprocated his comforting gesture and nudged King Braithwaite to do something. King Braithwaite then knelt and screamed sending orange energy that emanated from his body into the fallen trainer who began to vibrate uncontrollably. King Braithwaite stopped and stood up turning around to face Ravenous who was smiling.

"I see you have learned to control the energy within you, King Braithwaite. You too, have grown strong over the years!"

As King Braithwaite walked towards Ravenous with a smile on his face, the fallen trainer began to stir and then regained consciousness to his Howl's surprise. His Howl licked and nudged him with delight! Everyone above was amazed, even the chief magician and others were in awe.

"There was a window period in which I had to act and I just acted. Helleus was never fond of our armor. He always said that it was an excuse for necessary and unnecessary bloodshed. He was right! But even Helleus himself did not uncover the true secrets of the armor. I am only just beginning to discover its true power." King Braithwaite closed his eyes and went back in time for just a moment.

"Braithwaite, when we are done, what will become of our new race?" asked Ravenous.

"I will not lie to you Ravenous for that will be an insult. They will be used as means to an end," replied Braithwaite with a stone look on his face. King Braithwaite then shifted his attention to where King Gilleus and Bellorus were standing.

"That will not happen! Not by my watch," replied a stranger from behind everyone. His voice was clear and determined. His eyes were also on fire and his armor was burning strong and true just like King Braithwaite. His green hair blew with winds of energy that he had created by himself.

"Stop this madness, Braithwaite! This time, you have gone too far," replied Tereartre Levon who calmly walked past the two Kings and all the magicians and jumped down to meet the warriors below. The magicians could not believe that a warrior would be so skilled to slip past every defense that they had set up to prevent that from happening. Even King Gilleus was surprised but he knew Tereartre's reputation and smiled with his arms folded just watching everything transpire before him. Watching and waiting!

"TEREARTRE LEVON, a face indelibly etched in my memory. You have not aged a bit, still youthful and still strong. Haha! But I always wondered, who was the stronger, you or Gilleus?"

King Gilleus then jumped down from the top as well hitting the ground hard. He was kneeling on one leg with his head down smiling. He then lifted his head and screamed releasing the Hidamen Dark Knight power within and firing his eyes up. His armor flew in fast and painfully fused to his body in a haze of red and orange hues. He stood behind Tereartre Levon just making sure he wasn't going to do anything stupid. This was the first time in ages since King Gilleus released his Dark Knight power.

King Bellorus was surprised. It was the first time he saw it himself.

"So Tereartre Levon shows himself once again and disturbs our little bout. How rude!" King Braithwaite then faced Ravenous, "Sorry Ravenous, maybe next time." King Braithwaite showed a slight tinge of annoyance and disappointment with not getting the opportunity to fight with Howlen King.

Tereartre Levon banged his head and drew his sword out by placing his four fingers on his forehead. It was a flaming green color breathed in a yellow flash of flame; quite an elegant sword for quite a deadly man!

"Higardo and the Howls are creatures of the world that you have twisted and manipulated for your sinister purposes. Not to mention, casting the Minotaurs out of their own home. Did you think I was going to let that go? I will free them into the lands were they belong."

At that very moment, King Gilleus unleashed his deep orange sword of flame and power from his forehead and stood firmly between Tereartre and Braithwaite.

"This does not concern you Gilleus, if you respect life and this world, you will leave us be," commanded Tereartre.

"It does concern me Tereartre, for I am partly responsible for the creation of the Howls."

Suddenly, Ravenous lunged forward for King Gilleus who lifted his black and orange-flamed sword from his head to block the sharp claws that had attacked him. King Gilleus fell to the floor with Ravenous on top of him glaring at his fangs.

"Is that true King Gilleus? IS IT TRUE?"

Gilleus pushed his sword up sending Ravenous flying into the air some distance away.

Ravenous landed on his feet though and was preparing for another attack when Gilleus spoke out, "YES, it is true, you were created for the sole purpose of war," shouted King Gillues.

Ravenous growled at Gilleus's fateful declaration. Ravenous hurled himself at Gilleus but King Braithwaite intervened punching the angry Howl straight into the ground with bare fire fists.

"Ravenous, have you ever wondered who really killed Helleus Kendor?"

Ravenous's head lifted as he closed his mouth filled with fangs.

"Why are you so quiet Tereartre? Why don't you tell Ravenous about the night on top of Mount Killithur," motioned King Braithwaite.

Tereartre Levon stood silently with his head bowed looking deep into the ground.

Ravenous looked at Tereartre with horror in deep Saturn-brown eyes. The realization, the possibility had just hit him.

"No Tereartre! No! You couldn't have! I don't believe it! You were Helleus's best friend. You could have never taken his life. Never!" asked Ravenous with a sad and disappointed look on his face.

Tereartre looked up with regret and tears in his sunken neon-green eyes, "I had no choice, Ravenous. I was requested to do so by Helleus himself, to dispatch him while he still had a shred of sanity left within him, Ravenous," replied Tereartre with a deep sense of guilt in his eyes as he bowed his head in shame.

"WHAT!" shouted Ravenous and Gilleus, collectively. King Gilleus knew that Tereartre had killed Helleus but he didn't know the details and he didn't want to believe it.

"Helleus Kendor was not suffering. That is a lie, Tereartre! He was perfectly fine," replied King Gilleus waiting to strike Tereartre with his drawn sword, which slowly started to ooze flames of anger and fury.

"Braithwaite knows exactly what happened to Eric and how the events led up to me killing our beloved leader, Helleus. Why don't you tell them, Braithwaite? Tell them how Eric tried to kill us all, starting with the head of our order."

King Braithwaite looked at Ravenous and Gilleus and stood quietly.

"Tell them, Braithwaite!" Tereartre was waiting with gritted teeth. Braithwaite gritted his teeth as well knowing that he was going to have to tell them the truth sooner or later.

"Helleus killed Eric alright! I still don't believe Eric lost his mind. That's my brother you talking about Tereartre, my brother! He was one of the strongest among us. I still find it difficult to believe what you saying and I still won't believe it!" replied Braithwaite clenching his fists and gritting his white sharp teeth.

"WHAT DO YOU MEAN!" shouted Ravenous and Gilleus collectively again.

"It's true! Helleus dispatched him. Ravenous, wanna know why you're dead," replied Braithwaite with a very sad look on his face. King Braithwaite had his head bowed and did not utter a word eventually falling to the floor beginning to weep as he buried himself in his hands sobbing tears of sadness.

Ravenous turned to Tereartre for more answers, "Tereartre, you still did not say why you killed my former master," asked a very angry Ravenous.

"I will tell you that story another time, Ravenous," replied a firm Tereartre.

"You will tell me that story NOW, Tereartre!" replied the Howlen King.

He was livid! A fight was about to break out between Ravenous and Tereartre when the weeping of King Braithwaite interrupted them again.

ear of tears

King Braithwaite wept and wept to know that he could not bring back his brother. It was odd and strange for everyone to see the Lord of Sarcodia break down before them. The others saw this broken man kneeling on the ground with his head held in his hands and wondered what had really transpired. They all felt very sorry for him except for Tereartre who knew something more than the others about what really happened. The arena was filled with an air of sadness emanating from King Braithwaite. Throughout all the years of his life, he had only shed tears on two occasions, when his wife passed away and now when he recollected his thoughts about the death of his brother. He was an emotionally inhibited person and found it difficult to express his feelings openly.

King Gilleus was about to approach him when suddenly and completely out of the blue something clicked within King Braithwaite. A sharp pain shot into the back of his head causing him to scream out loudly sending him reeling with shock into the ground. The fire from his eyes intensified as he writhed in pain on the floor clutching at the loose sand that was available to him to grapple on. The energy he was creating was enormous, far greater than the normal amount a Dark Knight would usually generate when attracting the Hidamen armor to his body.

Tereartre, Gilleus, and Ravenous were in awe and were shocked at what was transpiring before their very eyes. They had never seen nor experienced anything like it before and it made them just a little nervous.

King Braithwaite then began to let out screams from the very core of his being and then he muttered the words of another language before regaining some composure and control over his body. His eyes stopped flaming for a moment and he managed to catch a glimpse of the warriors in front of him.

"Fri- - -ends, tell, tell my daughter and my son..." King Braithwaite felt exhausted and winded and gasped for air. "Tell them, I love them very much and that I am sorry." He then threw his head back again and screamed out loudly releasing a massive burst of energy that blasted everyone onto the floor. The ceiling started to cave in and the magicians made a run for it including King Bellorus, who felt he would no longer be of any service to anyone, also darted for the exit.

Ravenous motioned for the trainers and their Howls to get out while they still had the chance.

Tereartre Levon went deeper into the arena and made sure that no one was left behind.

King Gilleus held up parts of the ceiling to ensure a safe escape for those remaining trainers and howls.

King Braithwaite was going berserk!

Tereartre tried to get close to him but the energy blasts that he was emitting were far too strong for him to overcome.

The whole place was falling apart and neither Gilleus nor Tereartre could stay any longer. They jumped up into the royal chamber and then onto the roof and off the side of it for it was also caving in. They fled to the clear surface of daylight as the entire Sarcodian royal chamber caved in. The entire underground arena was now destroyed as the blue skies above shone brightly. Who knew if the magicians and other howls made it but they were clever folk and somehow they would have found a way out of the crumbling structure. Perhaps, that is what they longed for, freedom, thought Tereartre. Tereartre and Gilleus wiped the sweat from their eyebrows and sighed with relief. They felt no presence of Braithwaite and assumed that he was killed in his fit of rage and despite the hatred that Tereartre had for him, he still bowed his head in respect for his fallen comrade.

King Gilleus did the same.

The day was very beautiful and everyone including the Howls wondered why they were cooped up underground.

All the people of Sarcodia were on edge and wondered why the royal chambers had just caved in with their beloved leader still trapped in it.

Then, "What were those sounds emanating from underground," thought Ravenous. The howls answered their curiosity by growling from the depths of the cave. Then, one by one, Howls emerged from the ground with pride and fearless stone faces as they returned the stares given to them by nervous and afraid onlookers. Although very much afraid of them, the people of Sarcodia marveled at the creatures who marveled back at them. As more and more Howls emerged from underground, the people of Sarcodia backtracked and eventually retreated into their houses for fear of being attacked. Initially, it was thought that only a few Howls were created; however, the number that emerged suggested a different story. Only a few playful and fearless children remained. A young boy cautiously walked up to a Howl, taking great care not to provoke the foreign creature. He began to stoke its monstrous snout and to the surprise of the Sarcodian people, the creature did not retaliate. The young boy smiled but soon his smile was interrupted by the sudden change in the weather, which was very unnatural, almost magical.

Rainclouds and thunder had suddenly set in, taking the place of the cotton clouds and patchy blue hues in the skies. The earth below then began to quiver and shake.

"GET BACK!" shouted Tereartre who pushed all the people away from the void of rubble that was beginning to give way beneath them. Suddenly, the jagged rocks were blasted high into the sky and turned into deadly projectiles as they made their way back down to earth. The Howls saw fit to use their capabilities to protect the people from the deadly rocks. They armored themselves and shielded the vulnerable people that were close by with their bodies. The rubble simply ricocheted off them.

Tereartre and Gilleus saw fit to change into their Dark Knightean forms.

King Gilleus shouted and attracted his armor to himself but made sure that no piece of it killed anyone in the process and so did Tereartre. They were learning to intercept the Dark Knightean armor in its pathway to them. They began assisting in destroying some of the rock projectiles, which strayed too close to the innocent people with their swords.

The people of Gillmanor and Sarcodia did not yet realize that the man underneath the Dark Knightean armor was really their king. The attraction of armor was that fast. Once the people were secure and the dust had settled, an edginess filled the air with tense energy that pierced the very core of every Howl and man alike.

Someone was coming! Someone very powerful!

Slowly, the silhouette of a large dark figure arose from the ashes and dust below. It was winged and breathed in flame. Then its full appearance was revealed as the dust and smoke cleared around it.

Prince Bartholomew had come to see what was happening. The Prince's curiosities about his father were satisfied, only to find to his horror, a transformed version of him levitating in the air. It was King Braithwaite himself! His eyes were closed, but the energy he was emitting was incredibly awesome. All the common people could feel his presence and the combination of fear and overwhelming power brought them to their knees in the prostration of this proverbial "God" amongst them. Some women began to faint whilst some men began to backtrack with their families in tow, sensing an evil feeling about this new being before them.

Tereartre and Gilleus took a few steps back to examine the monstrosity before them. They were both intrigued and pensive! They had never seen anything like it before. Tereartre began to consider the possibility that each Dark Knight takes on a unique form once he or she reaches a new level in terms of strength or knowledge and eventually transcends into a higher-order being. He witnessed it first-hand with Eric and Helleus. Eric had a unique ability to go underground with ease like a Serpentine, which made him difficult to track whilst Helleus became so powerful, like a raging Bararg that he could not be stopped and the only way to stop him was to kill him.

Ravenous growled and didn't like it one bit. They were in trouble and he knew it.

King Braithwaite then opened his eyes sending an energy wave that threw everyone to the floor except the three strongest warriors in the front, Tereartre, Gilleus, and Ravenous.

All the Sarcodian elites were now on the frontline with these three warriors. All their swords were drawn despite the shock of seeing their king in this new form. Braithwaite's body was a dull, cold grey shade. His muscles rippled as he floated in the air with his wings neatly tucked in behind him.

Tereartre was the first to speak to him, "What happened Braithwaite? Who are you now?"

"WHO AM I? What a poignant question! Who am I? This a question we should all ask ourselves now and then. Who am I? Call me what you will! What I am is who I am and I have transcended, Tereartre. I am a High Dark Knight, as you would call us."

Tereartre and the others swallowed hard.

"You do not believe me!" replied King Braithwaite who clenched his fist sending out another energy wave that grounded everyone except Tereartre, Gilleus, and Ravenous. This energy wave was much stronger and ever-increasing in power.

Ravenous gritted his sharp teeth and finally yielded to the immense pressure and found himself now on his knees in pain. King Gilleus was also beginning to feel heavier and so was Tereartre. Finally, all succumbed to the awesome might of this new form of King Braithwaite and fell to the ground gasping for air and completely exhausted. Tereartre Levon looked up to find Braithwaite hovering just in front of him with his hands crossed and a smug smirk upon his face. Braithwaite touched the bottom of Tereartre's chin slowly lifting him up and off the ground with just two of his fingers. King Braithwaite then brought him closer to his face and whispered into his ear, "Tell Vallentorvan and the rest of this world, that a High Dark Knight has been born again and all those who oppose him, will perish! Do that! Now that I am whole, I will act with conviction and purpose. I am the fear in your hearts and I will be the undoing of the Dark Knightean Order. The son of Helleus Kendor will be the first to perish!"

Tereartre did not struggle as he was completely immobilized by the immense power of Braithwaite. He couldn't feel his entire body. He felt nothing! Then, King Braithwaite released him by throwing him to the ground to where King Gilleus and Ravenous were lying clutching the crumbled earth beneath them. Tereartre slid on the ground coming to an awkward halt just in front of Ravenous and Gilleus.

King Braithwaite then addressed the frightened people of Sarcodia, "Good people of Sarcodia! I will not burden you with idle talk." His voice beamed around his kingdom loudly. "My actions speak louder than my words. I officially relinquish control and leadership of my beloved kingdom to my daughter, Melody Griffin Braithwaite. I will go now to Mount Killithur." King Braithwaite then spread his translucent wings and took off disappearing into the clouds which cleared just as fast as they had arrived showing the original appearance once again.

Once King Gilleus regained his composure and footing. He stood up and looked into the sky where King Braithwaite flew into and wondered about the future of the world now that this new being was born into it. He then snapped out of his daydream and came to Tereartre's aid and so did Ravenous. They helped him up to his feet.

"Well, that settles that. I'm no longer interested in joining a psychopathic High Dark Knight club on some idealistic crusade of death! Friends again?" asked King Gilleus smiling at Tereartre who smiled back at him.

"Friends! Were we ever enemies?" Tereartre shook his head with relief and shook King Gilleus's old but strong hands.

"What now, Tereartre?" asked a very concerned King Gilleus. "We don't stand a chance against that!"

"The man is strong now! The last time I felt that much of presumably Hidamen's power was when his brother and Helleus lost it and transcended. Vallentorvan has most likely already felt the presence of King Braithwaite. That power was far too strong to miss. Gilleus, my friend, things are about to get very interesting!"

The Master unleashed

"So what do we know of? We have seen spiritual power in the form of the invisible Spireneé. We have seen wars waged only within the mind. We have seen the union of these elements and many other variations. What's the next step? A world without senses cannot be perceived in any way imaginable but if we knew that such a world existed, we still would not be able to comprehend nor recognize it, then would that world truly exist? Would we still exist? Would we and our so highly intellectual understanding of the world exist? The next frontier is the next understanding that does not rely on sensory information but on a higher spiritual plane that can be attained but not recognized in any sensual way. Let me explain, if you can see it, then it's not there. If you feel it, then you've felt nothing. All your senses must be in tune with each other and yet, not be used to attain the higher state of being. A higher state of being will simply not rely on sensory information to exist. It will exist with its frame of reference but not in our sensual frame of reference because it won't be based on anything we can identify with. Instead, it would be based on something else. But then, what is it based on if not on something identifiable, you may ask? If you can't perceive it in any way, then how can it exist, and yet it is there, among us, waiting to be discovered? How will we know what we're looking for, if we can't use our senses to find it? I'm saying, don't discard your senses, put them down for a brief moment in time and space and allow a different type of existence to prevail over your sensual desires. This is the mistake, many great meditators make. They try to run off using the power of their minds but the recognition of perception is the flaw in their technique. This is the foundation of just being. So now, come back, think, feel, taste, touch, and hear your world and revel in it. People misinterpret the notion put forth as not thinking or not using their senses, which is wrong. I'm saying, use your senses without using them. Slowly, you will begin to understand the higher plane of existence because as your senses increase in power, so too will your understanding and thinking processes. The spirit exists when you don't will it. It just surfaces naturally and spontaneously when you are at peace with yourself. The power is within you, Valkin! Realize it and utilize it to the fullest of its potential. You see Valkin, the balance of power," replied the master as Valkin awoke from his deep meditation on the shores of Gilipriel. "That is the true form of being. Soon, you will realize this form. Come, we have much work to do."

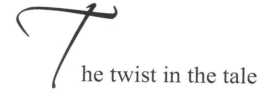

The twist in the tale

"An awakened Dark Knight you say. Of all the things one could ever fear, this is the one thing I feared the most! I'm sure that the news has spread all around this world of ours that King Braithwaite can no longer be controlled. It has indeed reached my ears and given me a very heavy heart. Come friends, rest now!" motioned a very concerned Vallentorvan as he breathed in and sighed.

Rufor booked his place near the fireplace of the Hallucagenian meeting room whilst Tereartre and King Gilleus seated themselves at the points of the triangular table facing Vallentorvan at the head point. Marve sat between Tereartre and King Gilleus.

Ravenous sat alongside Rufor and also stared deeply into the fire.

Rufor broke the silence first between himself and Ravenous. "So, when did they acquire my blood and that of Higardo's?"

Ravenous looked at him and replied, "When Rehowlor attacked you. He swiftly drew blood from your unconscious body with a device created by the Sarcodian magicians."

Rufor nodded his head and creased his lips conceding to the facts with some anger and frustration. He went back in time remembering how he was blasted back by the might of Rehowlor. It hurt his body and thoughts, so he snapped out of the recollection quickly.

"Well, that's it then, there's no hope! Pardon my pessimism good kings but I don't see any way to stop the being he has become now. He is just too powerful! Even if we marched with our full strength, we wouldn't stand a chance against him. He'll kill us all in his fit of rage," replied Marve with an air of defeat in his voice.

King Gilleus rubbed his hooked beard as his hazy blue piercing eyes shifted their gaze to Vallentorvan expecting a response from him. The red warrior sat quietly contemplating their next move.

"That's true, we don't stand a chance and if we take all our men and make a great war, they will perish along with us. That's something, I will not allow while this body still draws breath and remains sane."

Rufor got up and walked towards the table and rested his paws on the brown table surface. His silhouette flickered with the firelight on the table's surface. He looked around him and spoke out clearly. "Our hope lies within ourselves and our friends. My wolven ears have heard the biddings of two evil harbourers of King Braithwaite."

King Gilleus clenched his fists and joined the conversation with his powerful voice, "King Revengor and Arnaiboa! The dragon and the serpent! Those two are still in league with Braithwaite."

"Yes Gilleus, their fear of Braithwaite's power has overcome their better judgment and their alliance with him remains true and is a formidable one; one that will be very difficult to break nor defeat. I truly believe that King Braithwaite will not attack us himself but he will allow his minions to carry out their bidding at will. Their actions cannot be predicted easily either. Look at what transpired in DallaVega! It's looking increasingly bleak for us rebels." Rufor looked at Vallentorvan intensely.

Vallentorvan was preoccupied with his thoughts as he found himself staring at the fire now. He rocked in his great chair back and forth a few times whilst the others waited for a reply. Finally, Vallentorvan cut the tension in the room with a long-awaited reply. "I do not have a choice, my good warriors. I must now invoke the code of battle and pray and hope Braithwaite accepts it."

What's important to you?

"When I was younger, Valkin, a so-called friend of mine pointed out the funny manner in which dressed when he came to visit me here in Gilipriel. Back in those days, the fashion trends on the island were long white robes and nothing more but everywhere else especially on the mainland, people were wearing flashy, fruity colors more than all the rainbows you could imagine. Haha! Ah yes! It was a spectacle indeed! It was nice! I never objected to the visage of such splendid beauty. Living on an island is a hard thing to do," reflected the master to an attentive Valkin.

They were standing on the shoreline facing the most beautiful tangerine orange sunset with touches of white gold and mild grey steel clouds.

"He tried to make me look like a fool in front of my other friends, who came from distant lands to rejoice and reconnect at a party I held on the island, by saying that the clothes I was wearing were outdated and dull!"

Valkin folded his hands and had a look of shock and disgust upon his face and listened further intently to the story the master was relating to him wondering how anyone could belittle such a little, big man.

The master briefly looked out deep into the horizon of the vast ocean that lay before him holding a walking stick with his two hands contemplating his response to the misguided so-called friend of his.

Valkin was quite surprised that the master would actually hold a party. One would never say that the master was the party type if you looked at him at first glance, thought Valkin.

"Well, what was your response, master?" asked a very curious Valkin cusping his hands expecting a fight as a response.

"I simply told him that it was one of the perks in life."

Valkin was a bit confused and his face showed it.

"Let me explain, Valkin. What I was actually referring to was not the way I dressed being a perk in life. I referred to the folly of my 'friend's' way of thinking. His shallowness was evident in his mind. Appearances to him were higher up on his priority list. Why else would he choose to ridicule me so much? Well, of course, the superiority complex is inherent within most kinds of animals. Everybody wants to assert his or her dominance or will upon others without the slightest care or consideration for the individual's feelings. A rather silly dispensation if you ask me." The master smiled as Valkin agreed with him seeing that it would be rather silly and stupid to ridicule the master. Did the friend have a death wish or something, thought Valkin.

"But master, your friend ridiculed you. He was supposed to be your friend but if he acts like that, then, he really wasn't your friend after all. He has no depth whatsoever. If he really was your friend I would think that he would have complimented you, not ridiculed you," replied Valkin who expressed his feelings without any remorse but called the story as he heard it.

"I could not say that to him, Valkin. He was still my friend. I did not want to hurt his feelings. I knew what I thought about it but I also knew that it was not up to me to enlighten nor judge him. I could handle it. Oh yes! I could and I did." The master had a sadistic smile on his face suggesting something sinister.

"What did you do, master?" asked Valkin with great interest.

"I dealt with him."

"What do you mean you dealt with him, master?" Valkin was shocked and stood in disbelief as the master smiled and then chuckled.

170

"No silly boy. It's not what you think. I was angry at the time and in my mind, I turned into a beast and leaped after him after he called me a coward. Of course, none of this ever actually happened in real life. It was all going on in my mind and so I ran up to him and kneed him in the face and punched him once. He never got up again. My other friends were there as well in my mind. They watched in horror as I smote his ruins upon the ground. I arose the champion of the fight! I said to my friends who were taking a few steps back now, 'You see what I really am, don't become me, I will take out anyone who gets in my way' and then I left never to see any of them again. But all of this remember, happened in my mind."

"Ok master, that's what happened in your mind but what really happened that day?"

"Oh! I said my goodbyes to all my friends including the 'shallow one' and we all went home. That was that!"

Valkin was a bit relieved and looked at the small man and wondered for a moment that this man was actually normal but in an extraordinary way.

The master reminisced for a while about the incident.

"Did you ever see them again, master?"

"No. Didn't want to. I soon realized that all of these gatherings were just charades of materialistic youth, something that I had outgrown a long ago without even realizing it." The master chuckled remembering the old days. "But it was good at the time, I guess. Such is the nature of life. People will come and go and some will leave good and bad memories behind. It's all up to us to see which ones we wish to keep and which ones we will discard. I always say if you can control your feelings, you can control the amount of influence others will have upon you. If you master your feelings, then no one can touch you."

"No master, some people are just inconsiderate, and usually they are the ones who can't think properly." Valkin clenched his fist.

The master patted him on his back motioning him to calm down.

"We cannot make others think the way we do, Valkin, nor can we claim that we think better or know better. Everybody's different. Yes, it is true that focusing solely on one's appearance is folly and not encompassing the true way of thinking but some people in this world think like this. They are entitled to. That is their right to their individuality. Maybe one day they will learn from guys like you and me about life and how another man thinks and then only they might change their thinking. There are many paths to new learning. May theirs be the smoothest! We bless them."

"Master, you're too good to be true!" Valkin shook his head and smiled.

The master laughed with Valkin.

"Hey, Valkin! Let me tell you one thing. I am good now because I know what it feels like to be bad and the worst of them all. You heard my thoughts. That was the kind of man I was. I've changed since then."

"The brothers said that you are the greatest teacher of the dark martial arts. No one could stand up against your technique. If your friends only knew how much power you weld within your body, mind, and soul they wouldn't dare insult you with such mundane comments?"

"Probably, but they didn't know and what they don't know won't hurt them right? Haha! I train and practice the arts for self-realization, true expression, and attainment of peace. Something you will learn in time as well, Valkin. It begins with service to others to give them an opportunity you've had and more. It begins with elevating your thinking to a level that is so radical and influential, it's almost unbelievable! It begins with your consciousness and the shifting of it towards your greater being, whatever that may be. This story Valkin, is universal and thus you need to know the mistakes of others so that you may not repeat them in your life. Valkin, your journey has just begun. Always ask yourself, what's important to you? The clothes you wear, the house you live in, or maybe the girl you run after."

Valkin pondered for a bit whilst the master revealed a brown wooden smoking pipe. He snapped his hands and a small flame lit the contents of the pipe, which presumably was some form of tobacco. The master blew out the white smoke and offered Valkin a puff.

Valkin took a deep puff and tasted the scented tobacco smell. It made him feel light-headed and very nice. He gave the master back his pipe and listened some more.

"You see, you can live a mundane existence if you choose. You can follow the other people in your life like a sheep or you can blaze the trail. You can show them the way."

Valkin took in a deep breath and smiled, liking the idea of leading people.

"That doesn't sound so bad," replied Valkin as the master gave him the pipe to take another puff but Valkin declined to feel that it was not for him.

"Yes, yes indeed."

Both the master and Valkin watched the sun go down in the west as the small waves rushed up the shore and receded repeating the cycle. The sound was so peaceful. It was divine in some way. Both warriors smiled and drifted off into an afternoon daydream.

The Code of Battle

The purple iris of his eye was revealed as he opened his dark eyelids. He adjusted his wings by folding them to sit properly on the flat rock that he now regarded as his new throne. He clenched his fists now and then and saw the purple veins running along his grey forearm, biceps, and shoulders joining those veins onto his chest which stretched out into a network of purple trees that pulsated with life and energy. The newfound power that surged throughout his entire body was unbelievable! He felt reborn again and fresher than a spring morning. He felt the warmth of the sun hit his face as he closed his eyes once again to soak up the rays that warmed his clean-shaven face. He licked his grey lips slightly and wondered what he could do now that he was alone for just a moment. A yellow robin-death bird flew nearby and caught his attention. He whistled softly wanting the bird to fly into his hands, which it did.

It was a pretty little thing and it showed no fear of him. It stood quietly in the palm of King Braithwaite's hand and then chirped now and then. King Braithwaite somehow saw the bird in a new light. He could see its veins and then flesh and then as he focused more he could see its energy form, the very essence of its life, a soul some call it. Others call it Spireneé.

He lifted his hand releasing the bird into the air. King Braithwaite looked up into the sky and as he looked forward again, he saw his loyal subjects appear before him, Kings Revengor and King Arnaiboa. He seemed pleased to see them.

"What news from DallaVega and Hallucagenia, good kings?" King Braithwaite's voice was softer and more peaceful now as compared to before he transcended when he lashed out at Tereartre and the Sarcodian people.

Revengor replied first to King Braithwaite's command. "I have received word, my Lord, that Vallentorvan wishes to invoke the code of battle to prevent unnecessary bloodshed."

"A wise move on his behalf and I accept the suggestion." Both Kings Revengor and Arnaiboa were not pleased and felt they needed to explain their feelings to King Braithwaite. Arnaiboa was the first to go with his hissing voice.

"My lord, I think that we should not sssssspare any of them for fear of another rebellion against us once we asssssssume control. They could mussssssster a large enough force and attack us when we leasssssst expect..." King Braithwaite cut Anaiboa off before he could finish his sentence.

"Did I not say that, I accept the proposition, Anaiboa?" There was no hint of annoyance in Braithwaite's tone of voice, just authority and an unspoken power that he knew he possessed which struck fear in the heart of King Anaiboa.

"Yes, my lord," replied a very embarrassed and unnerved Anaiboa.

"Then leave it at that!" King Braithwaite looked up at the sky shifting his attention away from the affairs of the world for a moment.

"I also have word from your daughter as well, my lord," replied King Revengor waiting for a response which he got.

King Braithwaite was up on his feet and walked down the three steps to face Revengor who was now the same height as him.

"How is my daughter?" he asked showing evident concern in his voice and face.

"She misses you my lord and is very sad about how things have turned out. She is not disgusted by you. She has mixed feelings, as your transformation has resulted in her release," replied a genuinely sympathetic Revengor.

"I see, and my son?" asked King Braithwaite.

"He is also somewhat sad my lord. He is neutral about the situation and has not made any alliances with the barbarians. He has herded the Howls and released them into the Pine forests. He has also made a motion for peace between Sarcodia and Hallucagenia. I am sure that Vallentorvan is aware of this and will no doubt accept. The war between Sarcodia and Hallucagenia has ended even before it has begun," replied Revengor with a sad look on his face.

"Is that so? I guess somebody needed to take my throne. Who better than one's daughter hey? Did you mind reading them, Revengor?" asked King Braithwaite.

"No my Lord, just their emotions. It is more accurate, my Lord," replied Revengor bowing low to King Braithwaite.

"Revengor, Arnaiboa. The war between Sarcodia and Hallucagenia may have ended but the war between true warriors is about to begin." Revengor had some more news to share.

"My Lord. There's just one more thing. We have heard that the sandstone portal Dynasty gates are restless these days, which can only mean one thing. Someone's going to go in there. Should we send in a small of our elite warriors to deal with that someone, my Lord?"

"NO, you will do no such thing!" replied King Braithwaite with urgency in his deep voice. "It is not my curiosity that keeps them alive, nor is this a game that I play. I really want them to strengthen themselves. At this very moment, they are too weak to pose a significant challenge to us. I am a true warrior and to fight them knowing this will be a breach of my code and I will regret it for the rest of my life. That is my code of battle."

King Revengor and Anaiboa smiled and admired their leader and bowed with respect.

*T*he Dark martial arts of Life and War

"Keep your hand straight when you punch but slightly bent Valkin or else you'll invite someone to break it and that's a good way to lose a fight," replied the master as he trained Valkin.

They went through this routine for about an hour before taking a break.

"Take a breather and come over here with me boy, I will show you a little trick. Do you see this tree over here?"

Valkin looked at the swaying palm tree slanting towards the calm ocean and nodded his head in agreement. "Flick it with your hand."

Valkin looked at the master funnily and was taken aback by the rather strange request.

"I'm not joking boy, flick it with your index finger."

Valkin cautiously flicked it. Nothing happened! The wind blew across the beach. The skies were blue and dotted by cotton clouds but absolutely nothing happened to that old palm tree. It was unperturbed and gently continued its swaying motion with the wind of the day. The master slowly directed Valkin aside and said, "No, no, you're doing it all wrong, like this."

Valkin put his hands on his hips expecting nothing to happen as well.

The master flicked the tree with his index finger and as Valkin had predicted, absolutely nothing happened. Nothing happened for a few seconds.

Valkin smiled and was about to laugh at the master who had his back turned on the tree facing Valkin holding his arms behind his back, also smiling.

Suddenly, the earth beneath the tree started to shake and it looked as if some invisible hand started to pull the tree out from the soft sand as if it was an unwanted weed. Unexpectedly, it was hurtled into the sky with such speed and force, that within a few seconds, it was completely out of sight.

Valkin's wide-open mouth suggested his state of shock and utter disbelief at what he had just witnessed. Valkin expected the tree to come back down but as it grew smaller and smaller in sight traveling further away, he realized that it wouldn't return.

"Come, follow me," motioned the master.

Valkin snapped out of his mesmerized state and followed the master. He looked at the short, old man and for a moment and contemplated the awesome power within this man. Valkin then began to realize that this man was on another level completely.

The master began his explanation. "Your body is the vessel for the action and it obeys your every command. You have four primary weapons namely: your two hands and legs. Any martial artist is centered around these weapons, Valkin. Master their usage and you will be well on your way to becoming a formidable force. However, behind these weapons of destruction and creation, there is an invisible energy, a vital life force called Spireneé. No one has seen it, but it is very tangible and can be felt and more importantly, controlled. You've felt it before, haven't you Valkin?"

Valkin tried to think back to the first time when and when he had felt such a force and then he remembered.

"Yes Master, I have felt it many times before. First in my dreams or nightmares, then, when I trained with the Death Brothers in the Room of Pain and when I ran with the Bararg King, Bruce."

"In your dreams. How interesting! Those are powerful vehicles, dreams! They can shape your destiny, you know. Channel them towards a good direction and who knows what you'll be capable of achieving, hey Valkin? Never stop dreaming. Make your dreams come true."

"I agree master," replied Valkin.

For a moment, the master then closed his eyes and fell into a deep slumber, just for a moment.

Valkin thought the old man had died and become a dead man walking gently swaying his body and so he decided to wake him up with the slightest of touches to his small shoulders.

Suddenly, the old man got up. "WHOA! Who took away the sun? Ah yes, energy, energy, dreams! By the way, thank you Valkin for bringing me back. Don't know what happened there. Yes, energy gives life to everything. I've said it before and I will say it again, often as not the things that have the most amount influence over us in this world are the things that we cannot see nor grasp in our infinite intelligence. That makes life mystical, magical, and powerful. A bit like a woman, I'd say. Haha! The sustainable attributes like her ability to take care of you and sire a family with you and take care of them, her ability to love eternally are essentially the most important and sustainable attributes that cannot be seen in her visage, Valkin. You only can see her potential to do such things for you and the relationship. She is energy with great potential personified. Understand?"

Valkin looked like he had finally discovered the secret to life after what the master had just shared with him.

"Yes master, I finally understand. The key to winning this war is finding a good woman."

"Valkin, I'm talking about energy over here. Stay focused and don't change the subject!"

Valkin was taken aback. He swore that it was the master who had changed the subject. He just smiled.

"But master it was you who…"

"Ah! Not another word. Let us begin. Okay, how did I push the tree?"

"With your hands master!"

"Ahh! Very good answer Valkin, but WRONG! I used Spireneé energy to do so, not much but just enough. Where did I get the energy from you may ask?"

"From all around us," replied Valkin waving his arms and pointing to his surroundings.

"Ahh! Very good answer Valkin, that's correct! Energy is everywhere, all we need to do is learn how to channel it but how do we channel energy itself?"

"With our intention to do so," replied Valkin.

"Very good Valkin. A union between mind, body, and soul is required to create the right intention. We have spent much of our time, meditating, and not for nothing but to bring about this intention. You will now try to move the tree first with touch and then without touch."

They went to another tree that was located next to one that the master had uprooted and stood by it. Valkin examined the gaping hole in the ground left after the violent uprooting of the palm tree and looked at the master momentarily, who was examining the tree, and wondered again how such a little man could get this powerful.

The master turned around and looked straight at Valkin. "I train hard and I live and breathe for this life that I have been granted. That is how I do it!"

Valkin bowed his head with embarrassment and refocused his attention on the tree before him. He took a deep breath and exhaled widening his legs.

"Breath in the Spireneé all around you! Feel it become part of you and then move it to your hands."

Valkin closed his eyes and obeyed the master's commands.

"When you are ready, release it upon the tree before you without a word nor sound coming out from your mouth. Just release it. How will you know when to Valkin? Trust me, you will know. You will feel when your inner energy has exceeded the energy existing within the tree. Then, that will be the right time to strike."

Valkin delved deep into his core being, his consciousness, and felt a tingling sensation overwhelm his body like the feeling he had felt before when he last trained. The difference was, this time he wasn't stressed out. He felt very calm and cool.

The master smiled monitoring the rise in the boy's energy levels. The master's smile turned into intrigue. An energy field was beginning to form around Valkin, which was contrary to the fact that energy could not be seen with the naked eye. This field was very visible forming a blue-hazy color with yellow streaks of energy flickering out from it here and there. The yellow streaks of energy then transformed into occasional outbursts of fire that darted from the blue hazy sphere around Valkin.

The master sensing that this was quite enough energy then gently delved into Valkin's mind and told him to release the energy he accumulated.

Valkin opened his eyes and flicked the tree.

There was an immediate response that first uprooted the tree and sent it flying forward and then upwards into the sky. At the same time, the tree that the master uprooted came back from its journey into the sky landing right on the same spot that it was evicted from earlier.

Valkin had to snap out from his trancelike state to avoid being hit on the head by the incoming tree.

The master smiled. "Very good Valkin. You have done it. I must say that your energy is unlike any I've ever encountered before. But then again, each individual has his or her unique manifestation of energy. It can manifest in many different forms."

Valkin was quite pleased with himself after the master's complimented him. The master then turned his attention to the fallen tree that was lying on its side looking exhausted and almost dead.

"Now it is time for healing and planting. Give me a hand over here Valkin. This palm tree is tired and wants to go back into the ground."

The master than did something truly remarkable. He picked up both trees and struck them into the ground as if they were mere seedlings. He then closed his eyes and began to cement the roots back into the ground using some of his life force to breathe life back into the trees. Valkin was amazed and wondered how the master could achieve such a special feat.

The sunset on Gilipriel was a great backdrop for the rekindling of life.

Showdown at Gilipriel

The moon was high and the island was quiet. Only the rhythmic pattern of small waves washed up on the shore with a swish and sway in the pale blue moonlight. Valkin was fast asleep but the master was wide awake. He stood by the entrance to his humble hut looking at the moon above the shoreline, just observing it through the thin slit of his visage. He felt that someone was around and he smiled and closed his eyes.

"I HAVE RETURNED, AS PROMISED! WHERE IS THE BOY, MASTER?" An aged but powerful voice called out from the distance.

The moonlight became stronger as the full moon stood high above the shoreline on this clear and bright night masking the face of the stranger. The birds of Gilipriel rustled and stirred from their high perches atop the trees that began to gently sway with an approaching wind. The silhouette of a dark figure was approaching from the sea. He was hovering towards the shore at a very slow pace stirring up the water below with his incredibly strong energy signature. He then touched down on the sand with his bare feet. He stood silently and waited patiently for a response from the master who was still standing by the entrance of his hut. The eyes of the stranger scanned the island looking for signs of life. It wasn't long before Zeldor, the Lizard King arrived to meet the stranger. Zeldor hissed loudly and was about to attack him when another strong voice rained out across the island.

"Stand down, Zeldor!" It was the master's voice. The master then stepped out to personally greet the stranger.

He was not alone!

Valkin had gotten up by that time and realized that someone was outside. He quickly slipped into his gear and followed the master wearing his full black fighting outfit, the same that the Death brothers wear, carrying his blue-orange sword at his side. Valkin looked at the dark figure before him in the distance trying to make him out but he couldn't. The moonlight was far too strong tonight making the stranger's face too difficult to see.

"It has been a long time, hasn't it my student?" asked the master.

"Yes my master, it has!" replied the stranger bowing. The winds on the island began to pick up again but this time their intensity was reaching that of a gale-force nature. The beach sand was being picked up by the wind and began blasting the master and Valkin who narrowed their visages of the stranger but still stood firm. "I apologize for my abruptness, I've come for the boy, my master!"

"Before you even attempt to take him, why don't you introduce yourself properly to him first? I taught all of my students to have manners if I remember correctly!"

The dark figure then bowed and walked forward to face Valkin. His hair was a bushy white and his body looked frail and old up close. His beard was white and his eyes were a stable steel grey color that glowed in the moonlight. He smiled at Valkin and stretched out his hand to shake Valkin's hand.

"My apologies for being so rude! Rehowlor is my name, former student of the master, Wind, and Lightning elemental and leader of the Elemental Force. It is an honor to finally meet you Valkin, son of Helleus Kendor."

"Likewise, Rehowlor. I heard you caused quite a storm some time back at Hallucagenia?" replied Valkin who also smiled and shook his hand.

Rehowlor smiled and stepped back and looked at the short figure of the master leaning forward on his walking stick with a hunched back.

"So my reputation precedes me. Yes, the Hallucagenia incident! I did have a lot of fun but I was quickly put into place by another if you can recall?"

"Sorry, I didn't get to see your moment of glory. I wasn't conscious at the time to gather all of the details," replied Valkin.

"That's too bad, boy. You missed the best parts. Anyway, I have no other choice but to dispatch you right here and now before King Braithwaite gets a hold of you. I am so sorry my master. This must be done! We have no other choice. Death by hand is as good as death by King Braithwaite's hand"

"That's a bunch of nonsense Rehowlor and you know it! You are just scared, that's all. Leave us alone to train and go back to Groudenor, Hyedrasor, and Falkarnor. Maybe not Falkarnor, he's out of action for now. I heard they put him in his place back at Hallucagenia. You know, everybody who goes to Hallucagenia always seems to come out of that place more humbled than when they came in and still the people just don't learn to leave the barbarians alone," smiled the master.

"You've always had a wonderful sense of humor master. Don't push me too hard though. You may succeed in getting me angry and we all know what happens when I get angry?"

"You get winded," replied the master out of the blue.

Valkin then looked at the master who looked back at him and then they both looked at Rehowlor and started to giggle. Rehowlor became very annoyed and more agitated.

"Still full of jokes! You don't expect me to believe that the vessel I see before me is capable of withstanding the true power of an elemental, let alone that of an awakened Dark Knight."

"Rehowlor! This is no empty vessel. I have full confidence in my newly trained warrior, Valkin. Do not insult any further or face my wrath!"

Valkin was a bit amused with the flying remarks of cynicism and philosophy. He quite enjoyed it! He also appreciated the master's defense of his abilities.

"We shall see!" Rehowlor turned around and walked to a larger clearing on the shoreline away from the master's hut.

The master turned to Valkin and whispered into his ears, "The stage is set! Now, don't let me down, son!"

"The last time someone said that to me, I was thrown into a situation I didn't want to be in," replied a somewhat concerned Valkin.

"Oh well! In that case, I shouldn't say this..." replied the master with a fake look of concern as he shook his head and looked at the sand.

Valkin was in too much suspense not knowing what the master was about to say.

"...Shouldn't say what master?" asked Valkin wanting to know the answer to that question.

"Good luck kid, I should have told you this earlier, Rehowlor is actually the strongest student I ever had!"

Valkin's mouth was wide open with a newfound fear that began to paralyze him.

"Come along now, don't keep him waiting. He gets very impatient as you can see and then becomes even more powerful."

Valkin's face was filled with even more fear as he turned around and walked towards Rehowlor who had his hands folded. As Valkin got closer, Rehowlor stretched his hands forward and broke his knuckles warming up for what promised to be a very interesting fight.

"Relax kid, when you relax you won't feel the pain too much, you'll just accept it!" replied Rehowlor.

The master's smile then turned into a very serious look as Valkin pushed the sand in with his heavy spring forward towards Rehowlor...

*T*he code of battle is invoked

Vallentorvan wore a bright white tunic with a long blood-red coat over it. His long reddish hair flowed onto his shoulders as his black boots singed the ground leading him up the gravel steps to greet King Braithwaite who was standing in front of his throne waiting to receive him. There was a huge boulder of rock behind his throne. King Braithwaite's now grey hair blew softly on this beautiful day with the gentle breeze in the air.

Tereartre Levon was on Vallentorvan's right and King Gilleus was on Vallentorvan's left. Tereartre was in his usual Werethallic outfit and King Gilleus was wearing his orange and red tunic with red leather pants.

King Braithwaite smiled and then laughed as the three stopped before him. "You know Gilleus, I've always thought that the clothes from Gillmanor looked ridiculous but I did not have the heart to tell you that at first!"

King Gilleus burst out in laughter and so did Braithwaite! After a few minutes, they managed to compose themselves and King Gilleus replied, "You know Braithwaite, you got that right! AARRRHH!" King Gilleus let out a powerful scream and clenched his fists as he gathered energy toward his body. The armor of death flew onto him from all directions fusing with the pressure points within his body. The chest piece unexpectedly caught Braithwaite off his guard on his cheek on its journey toward King Gilleus's body. It made a perfect slit on the former Sarcodian King's cheek. Purple blood oozed from the small wound on Braithwaite's pale face. A drop of blood fell to the ground causing some dust to be ruffled up into the air. Just a few seconds after, the slit began to close and heal completely. Tereartre noticed this as King Gilleus completed the assembly of the armor of death onto his body. His eyes flamed fire through his helmet and his sword glowed red-hot as he held onto the handle tightly.

"It's been a long time. I've forgotten how good it feels to be a Dark Knight again!" replied King Gilleus.

King Braithwaite smiled and shook his head in agreement, "And what about you, Tereartre Levon?" asked Braithwaite with genuine interest.

"In time, old friend, in time but we must first deal with the issue at hand." Tereartre's smile was slight and ominous. King Braithwaite shifted his gaze to Vallentorvan who had his head bowed slightly. Vallentorvan did not make any eye contact with Braithwaite yet. After a brief moment of silence, he spoke with his head still down, "I came here to invoke to code of battle to prevent unnecessary bloodshed to my people. Do you accept my proposition, Braithwaite?" Vallentorvan finally looked up at Braithwaite waiting for an answer from the winged man that stood before him.

"I accept your proposition." Vallentorvan bowed and then turned around to walk away when out of the blue, King Braithwaite clapped his hand sending a thunderous shockwave of energy that rustled the dust of the earth for miles and miles on. "Only on condition that it is effective immediately!"

Upon that declaration, Revengor and Arnaiboa walked out from behind the boulder and stood next to Braithwaite. "Do you accept my proposition, Burning Desire?"

Vallentorvan pulled out his lava sword from his heart as the lava began to flow from his eyes to his cheeks but never fell to the ground.

Tereartre Levon attracted the armor of death to his body as Revengor jumped up into the air to execute an aerial attack on Tereartre Levon.

King Gilleus eyed Arnaiboa who hissed at him raring for a fight.

Arnaiboa didn't waste any time. He dived into the ground making Gilleus hypersensitive to his surroundings.

Gilleus, held his sword tightly in his right hand waiting for Arnaiboa to spring out of the ground. He had his left hand cocked and ready to grab Arnaiboa whenever he decided to come out of hiding.

Revengor's fist then struck Tereartre's elbows hard pushing the Werethall King into the ground a bit.

Vallentorvan looked at Braithwaite who stared back at him. A stone behind Braithwaite fell and when it hit the ground, Vallentorvan and Braithwaite locked hands sending out a wind of energy, each trying to overpower the other with sheer brute force and power. Braithwaite gritted his teeth and stretched his wings backward trying to gain the upper hand but Vallentorvan held his ground.

Arnaiboa burst out of the ground behind King Gilleus and kicked his back sending him flying forward and burning some trees on his way into a nearby boulder which was obliterated as he crashed into it.

Arnaiboa went back into the ground smiling. King Gilleus gritted his teeth shook his head and raised his energy level shaking the entire ground. He then jumped up into the air and dived into the ground to snuff out Arnaiboa himself using the heat generated from his body to burn his way through. The ground was becoming unstable as a result but King Gilleus didn't care. This was a battlefield now and killing Anaiboa was all he cared about!

Tereartre regained his footing and hit Revengor's stomach hard causing Revengor to spit out some blood. Tereartre followed that up with a knee to Revengor's face causing the Razortorian king to fly into the air and hit the ground hard some distance away.

Vallentorvan and Braithwaite let go of each other and jumped back to a safer distance. Braithwaite punched his forehead pulling out a white sword that shone as brightly as the sun temporarily blinding Vallentorvan. Vallentorvan closed his eyes and when he tried to open them again, he couldn't. An incredible pain prevented him from opening his eyes. Braithwaite smiled and flew straight toward him intending to behead him with his awesome sword. At the very last moment, Vallentorvan lifted his sword to block the deadly stroke that sailed over his head. Braithwaite yielded his attack and then spoke, "I expected nothing less from Vallentorvan himself. I must ask you though, how does it feel to be two beings in one, Vallentor, or is it, Donavan?"

"It feels great, Braithwaite!"

Braithwaite's sword then disappeared from his hand at that declaration by disintegrating into thin air and vanishing. He pondered for a while on a thought and then looked at Vallentorvan. He called upon his other servants to stop fighting.

Revengor suddenly stopped as well as Arnaiboa and jumped to Braithwaite's side.

"You know, Burning Desire. We're playing games here you and I, both keeping each other alive, both reluctant to show his true hand. Why don't we give all of this up and project right to the end?"

Vallentorvan began to break into a very nervous sweat at Braithwaite's declaration. He wondered what he meant by that declaration...

Rehowlor vs. Valkin

As Valkin lunged forward, he withdrew his 4ft long sword and simultaneously thrust out a punch for Rehowlor's face but missed cleanly, as Rehowlor disappeared from Valkin's sight. Valkin's head then jerked backward and jolted forward as he got kicked from behind by Rehowlor's aged but strong foot. Valkin landed face-first in the sand, crashing and rolling into some palm trees flattening them. He pushed himself up quickly holding his back, which felt singed and painful. He shook his head free from the sand particles that clouded his vision whilst

Rehowlor prepared a bolt of lightning to strike Valkin with. Rehowlor acquired his white lightning in his right hand and hurled the deadly lightning javelin toward Valkin. It was going straight for Valkin's heart but surprisingly Valkin clad in full black caught the bolt just before it struck its heart target and held it for what seemed like an eternity in his left hand.

Rehowlor was both surprised and impressed at the young man's speed and strength to see such an attack coming toward him.
Valkin then held the bolt with his two hands and broke it in half releasing a thunderous clap that shook the earth a bit.

The master smiled and rested one hand on the other holding his walking stick.

Rehowlor put his head down and said, "I'm so sorry boy. It ends here and now! I'm not going to deliberate anymore. You're finished!" He flew up into the air and held his hands up high summoning a great storm that swirled round and round with lightning and thunder mixed with puffy grey and charcoal black clouds of fury.

Valkin looked up into the sky and felt a cold chill run down his spine. He realized that the attack that Rehowlor was preparing was meant to be a final killer blow to kill him and it didn't seem like the master was going to intervene.

Rehowlor continued to summon his ultimate attack, the eagle bolt of lightning. Slowly, it formed above the clouds and its bright silhouette started to become visible. Then, more formed above the clouds like torchlights waving through the air above the clouds.

Valkin began to stress a bit seeing the great yellow shadows of the giant 50 ft eagles above the clouds and the unearthly squawking of the creature created only to kill.

Rehowlor smiled as he looked down upon Valkin with his beady and condescending eyes. He knew the end was near and swallowed hard. There were ten, each flying out from the eye of the storm. One by one they merged to form a supercharged lightning eagle.

Valkin had never seen an eagle before but he heard stories about them. They were terrifying and awesome creatures. It screeched and hawked through the air like a caged beast waiting to attack its prey. Rehowlor put down his hands after completing the summoning and with the eagle he just summoned behind him, he looked at Valkin and said, "I hope you understand that by taking your life, others will stop fighting. YOU ARE JUST TOO DANGEROUS TO BE ALIVE, BOY! I hope that you find a way to forgive me."

Valkin didn't fully understand the meaning of Rehowlor's words but he knew that he meant every word and began to feel very wrong.

Rehowlor pointed his right hand to Valkin. At that signal, the eagle swooped down with lightning speed on Valkin and caught him with its huge claws. The eagle was very hot and began to burn Valkin's flesh as it flew high up into the sky.

Valkin winced in pain and let out a scream.

The master's eyes closed sensing that the boy was in danger but knew that he could not interfere in the battle. He inhaled and watched on.

191

The eagle stopped some ten miles above the ground and hovered for a few moments. It then wrapped its wings around its body and Valkin's and began to glow a white-yellow color, which lit up the entire shoreline of Gilipriel.

Rehowlor looked at the master and remarked, "I see your lack of intervention proves that this is the best course of action."

"The day I approve of taking a life needlessly will be the day that I die, Rehowlor. I just don't want to interfere for other reasons," replied the master who somehow also knew that the end was near for Valkin but still had hope. He could still feel the flicker of Valkin's life holding on like a dying candle flame dancing in the wind trying to stay alive.

Rehowlor looked on as the eagle sent out beams of lightning all around destroying the trees and sending up large volumes of sand and water high up into the air wherever it strikes. It finally reached a climax and exploded sending out vast plumes of smoke and dirt all around. The master closed his eyes and looked up into the sky taking a deep breath and as he exhaled, he felt the glimmer of Valkin's life vanish.

Raven was watching the entire ordeal from across the shore. He could not see the fight but he did feel it and he did see the final blast of light which worried him greatly for he too could not sense Valkin's energy trace anymore.

Rehowlor came down to earth again and walked up to the master extending a comforting hand to his shoulder and then walked on.

"Grrrr! Grrrr!" The gritting of someone's teeth was then heard. It was soft, yet audible from a distance. The gritting transformed into a low grunt. "Rahhhh!!! Rahhhh!!!"

Rehowlor slowly turned around as the master picked up his head to see the source of the strange sounds. Both could not believe their eyes. Flames were oozing out of the eyes of the mysterious dark warrior's helmet. No armor was seen on the warrior's body but the sword of black and orange flame was held tightly in his hands. His other sword had vanished and was now replaced by this one filled with flame and fury. His clothes were tattered and torn exposing his blood-stained body. The sand melted around him as he walked towards Rehowlor with his gaze fixed only on him. His breathing was deep and heavy as his pecks rose and fell with each breath rippling the muscles upon his larger and stronger body. He walked past the master who did not even flinch. Only the master's eyes followed the warrior. Rehowlor jumped up into the air and tried to summon another eagle but the warrior caught his leg as he tried to and held him tightly. Rehowlor struggled and struggled but the more he struggled, the tighter the warrior's grip got. The warrior's grip then began to burn Rehowlor's flesh deeply until the warrior flung Rehowlor to the ground in front of him. Rehowlor crashed into the sand and rolled many times before the momentum of the throw got exhausted causing him to finally come to a halt. Rehowlor looked up and tried to find the warrior but the warrior disappeared and reappeared in front of him gripping him by the scruff of his neck slowly picking him up and lifting him off the ground with one hand.

The warrior gritted and ground his teeth and lifted his sword touching Rehowlor's head once with it. He then touched Rehowlor's two shoulders and drew the sword back preparing for a final death stroke when the master suddenly appeared beside them. The Warrior swung his flaming sword nonetheless at Rehowlor who closed his eyes waiting for the inevitable to happen but just before the sword struck its target, the master held onto the sword from the opposite side with just his two fingers. The master seemed to be impervious to the scorching heat that the sword emitted. Amidst the heat waves, he calmly remarked, "VALKIN! That's enough!" Valkin stepped back loosening his grip on Rehowlor's neck and letting him fall to the ground. His neck was badly burnt and smoked a bit as it cooled down with the wind that he created.

"That's enough!" repeated the master.

Valkin tilted his head and looked at the master and spoke with an unusually deep voice, "Why is it enough when Rehowlor is so close to death and not when I am, master? Why must I die? What did I ever do to anyone?" The master kept quiet. "So it's true. You wanted me dead as well, master!"

The master looked up at Valkin and replied, "After all we've been through Valkin. Do you think I'm the kind of man who would allow my student to perish in front of my eyes?" Valkin screamed and shook his head showing how much he was struggling inside. He held his helmet and looked at the master, which had a calming effect on him. Valkin's fiery eyes cooled down as his helmet disintegrated into ashes and blew away with the wind.

193

The master turned to Rehowlor, "Thank you for coming. I appreciate it." Rehowlor got up and smiled.

Valkin was shocked. He realized only then, what had transpired.

"Thank you for making the visit worth my while, master. You were right about him. I guess it worked!"

"Mmmm! It would appear so. That was not even its true form, Rehowlor. I can't imagine the force he will become when he transforms fully."

Valkin was listening to the entire conversation because the master purposely allowed him to do so by speaking in his presence.

"Is it possible to teach him how to control it though, master?"

"Unfortunately, I can't. Only experience will serve him best. The Dark Knightean power is a beast that cannot be tamed by rigid technique. It is most effective when released. He needs to be around other Dark Knights as well. Perhaps they will help him to harness its true potential." Valkin continued to listen as he grappled with what had just happened to him.

"They are unfortunately a bit tied up as we speak, master!" replied Rehowlor.

"I know, I know," replied the master who held an ominous thought within his mind. Braithwaite has become very strong, I believe?"

"Yes, he has. I would go so far as to say that he has become almost a God, my Master."

"A god you say, Rehowlor! No man is a God, Rehowlor. Don't be too hasty to put him on that pedestal. There is a fight still left in some warriors. The protective shield around this island prevents Braithwaite's sight from reaching us."

"What does Braithwaite desire master?" asked Rehowlor with intrigue.

"I can't put my focus into it. I'm not sure what it is. He is a difficult man, to sum up, and that is what makes him so strong. All strong individuals are difficult, to sum up, Rehowlor."

"I find that quite surprising, even from you master, but alas I agree, even in his presence, it was very hard to figure out what he was thinking. What now, master?" The master turned to Valkin and then back to Rehowlor.

"Rehowlor, the boy's training with me has come to an end." The master looked at Valkin who was a bit shaken after the ordeal but still standing. He smiled and shook Valkin's hand. "Go get your stuff Valkin. It is time to go."

Valkin smiled and mixed feelings filled his heart about what he almost did to Rehowlor.

Rehowlor smiled and bowed his head accepting Valkin's non-verbal apology.

Valkin smiled and bowed to them and hurried away to get his stuff leaving Rehowlor and master alone to converse.

"This day's journey will be long and perilous. Revengor and Arnaiboa will no doubt be dispatched and they will hunt whoever roams near that pathway, Rehowlor. Once you fall into their clutches, I cannot guarantee your safety anymore."

"I understand master," replied Rehowlor.

"Did you sense his presence during the fight, Rehowlor?"

"No, I didn't," replied Rehowlor guessing what the master was thinking to ask.

"Very interesting, very interesting indeed!"

"Could you master?" The master narrowed his eyes and thought for a moment before he answered. He looked at Rehowlor who towered above his short stature and smiled.

"Short answer. No. Long answer. I don't know. Haha!"

Valkin finished packing his kit and ran out of the master's hut.

"Thank you master for training me. I wish to see you again. Take care." Valkin shook the master's hand and bowed in respect to him and walked towards the shore. He and Rehowlor floated away in the light air currents that Rehowlor generated. The master looked on as a dark figure approached him from behind. He wore a black, silky outfit and had short dark hair. His gleaming yellow eyes sent out a ray of light through the dark night. He came and stood beside the master and folded his arms remarking, "And so it begins…"

To be continued...

Valkin Kendor will return in
The Dark Knights Ascend

BOOKS IN THE OUTCAST SERIES

Click the image to begin your next journey...

BOOK ORDER IN THE OUTCAST SERIES

CHRONOLOGY: All stories in the Outcast of the Dark Knight series are shown in chronological order as follows:

The Dark Knights Return

The Dark Knights Sunrise

The Dark Knights Ascend

The Dark Knights Inferno

The Dark Knights Awaken

Book VI is coming soon!

BOOKS IN THE OUTCAST BOXSET SERIES

Click the image to begin your next journey...

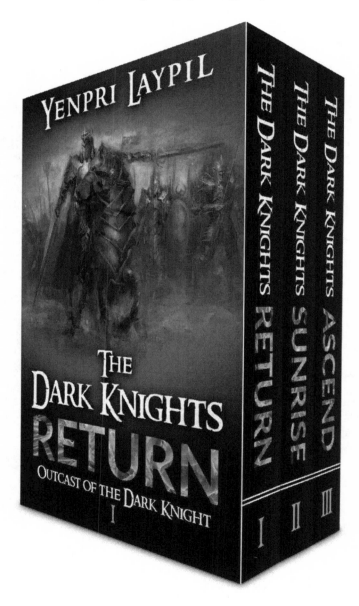

BOOK ORDER IN THE OUTCAST BOXSET SERIES

CHRONOLOGY: All stories in the Outcast of the Dark Knight series are shown in chronological order as follows:

Boxset 1: Books 1-3

Boxset 2 is coming soon!

Subscribe to my emailing list

Please sign up to be the first to receive news updates on new book launches and much more from me, Yenpri Laypil. Signing up gives you exclusive access to the announcement of new Fantasy Worlds, characters and sagas that I create for you.

Follow & Like Yenpri's Facebook Page

Click the facebook, twitter or youtube icons to navigate to each respective kingdom...

I respond to your messages and share content and sayings that engage and challenge your mind! I enjoy interacting with my readers, fans and followers whom I call my friends!

Made in the USA
Columbia, SC
26 June 2023